Claudia

Danyvid Olivares-Villagómez

Summer 2019

Last time I saw you
We had just split in two.
You were looking at me.
I was looking at you.
You had a way so familiar,
But I could not recognize,
'Cause you had blood on your face;
I had blood in my eyes.
But I could swear by your expression
That the pain down in your soul
Was the same as the one down in mine.

The Origin of Love
Hedwig and the Angry Inch
Stephen Trask

Dionisio, Claudia

Part 1

He was laying, eyes closed shut and groggy from the few coherent thoughts jumping in his mind. Dionisio was waiting for death to finally close the road of his short life. He was in his solitude; in the most intimate part of it. The hospital room was cold and the small blanket that the nurse provided to cover himself was useless.

The woman entered the room cautiously; she was not planning to surprise him, she simply did not want to wake him up in case he was asleep. He did not hear her when she stood at the bed's edge. Her breathing was intense and someone with all his working senses could have immediately sensed her presence. But not Dionisio. The Death was not going to concede anymore privileges. Softly, the woman reached with her hand to take his. She felt his bones, his wasting away, his coldness. At that moment, Dionisio recognized the touch of that skin, of that hand that he held many times, that many times he rubbed intentionally to be close to her. A woman's hand, tender but firm. He kept his eyes closed; he could not stand watching her face one more time, not during his last moments alive.

"Thank you for coming," he said in a deep, heavy, ill voice.

"I was not going to miss your death, I have lived a good part of my life with you, in your presence or absence. And it is important for me to be here." answered Claudia.

"And why this late? You should've come before when my hopes were still alive; what is left today?" Dionisio said with remorse.
Claudia reddened.

"I am here, and that should suffice."
The room grew silent, but their hands kept touching and rubbing each other.

"We are not going to fight the day you die." she said.

"Who says I am dying today?"

"I say that. I promised some time ago that the day you die, I would be beside you. Do you remember that? Today I am here and I doubt there is anything that can rescue you, there is no miracle to save you."

Dionisio moved his mouth trying to smile. Slowly, he opened his eyes to admire the reality in front of him: it was Claudia, in all her glory, always a girl in the process of becoming a woman. For a few seconds they looked at each other's eyes, both realizing that their reflections were just that: a reflection, a vision. Dionisio breathed with difficulty trying to gain strength, then he spoke softly as if praying.

"Come, get closer and kiss me on the cheek, the way I like it."
Claudia chuckled and said,

"You are incredible, you are this ill and you are still the same. Do you want to grab my ass as well?"

"If that is possible, of course!"

"You have no shame!"

Claudia knew him more than anyone, she knew his weaknesses and what made him happy. She got closer to kiss him on the cheek with open and moist lips, a lasting kiss. At the same time, Claudia took Dionisio's hand and placed it on the back of her thigh. Struggling, Dionisio moved his hand upwards to feel Claudia's ass, still firm and beautiful. A tear rolled down Claudia's cheek.

"You have no shame!" repeated Claudia.

"You know that I do it because you let me do it. I know you like it."

"It's mercy."

"That's a lot of time of your mercy! I knew you were heavenly, but I did not know you were a goddess."

Silence again. Claudia sat at the edge of the bed to watch the last moments of that man that she intensely loved and equally intensely detested. In her mind, she could see the memories when she first met him, of his arrogance to speak to her just in monosyllables, and his smile that she could never erase from her mind. But mostly, she could feel the familiarity of that man: the union between the two of them.

And that man got lost in an unsurmountable tiredness, taking him to the last dream of his life, a snow-covered meadow where buffaloes in the distance galloped powerfully. In the middle of the meadow, Claudia's silhouette called to him. Dionisio walked towards her, he was afraid but full of joy. Once he reached her, they held hands and kissed as if they were longtime lovers. They stood apart and she smiled at him showing her pearl-like teeth.

"Go," Claudia said, "and let us rest."

The moon rose on Dionisio's last last night on earth. Claudia left him to sleep and disappeared without saying goodbye.

Part 2

The October moon bathed Salamanca with
blue-hued rays. Those beams entered uninterrupted
into the houses and apartments through windows,
holes, and cracks, creating blue-hued shadows of
everything they touched. This moon was intense; it
was big as all October moons are. This moon created
larger and more ferocious tides than usual in the
oceans far away from Salamanca, but also it
produced tides of feelings and blood rushes, needs.
And all couples on that night living at the altitude of
Salamanca, closer to the sky, suffered an intense
desire to be even nearer to the one they love, the
moon rays and gravity serving as a celestial
aphrodisiac. Some kissed, some hugged, some made
love. One of those couples, among the moans and
sweat, created a new life: a small cell that used to be
an ovum, beginning the blueprints of a person.

The moon was a complete circle floating in the
July sky using its gravity to pull away prematurely
from his mother's womb a boy that looked more like a
bloody and beaten tadpole than a baby. The doctor
saw him and concluded that the kid was either dead
or close to it. But the boy was not dead, he was only
watching his mother through his closed and almost
transparent eyelids. His mother cried when the doctor
told her the baby was stillborn. Dionisio, still in the
doctor's hands, heard those words with his premature
ears and at that moment he decided to mock the
doctor. He thought about a survival plan and
demanded from The Death, that was hovering in the
corner of the room waiting impatiently, to take him at
a later date in the future. The Death winked an eye

and granted the request. Dionisio opened his eyes and pissed on the doctor's face.

Part 3

The Death conceded to allow Dionisio a breath of new life, but she was still The Death: mean and wretched. Did he think that The Death granted favors? No, The Death always takes something in return. She touched Dionisio's heart and made it weak, as a reminder that She was always around. Because of this touch, before he turned 2 years old, Dionisio became severely ill and ended up in the hospital for a few weeks. There, the doctors told Dionisio's parents, Mr. and Mrs. Diosdado, that their child had a rare heart defect that made it beat out of rhythm. The doctors had no knowledge of the cause of this condition nor how to cure it, but told Mr. and Mrs. Diosdado that moving to a lower altitude city, maybe somewhere at sea level, would help Dionisio's weak heart to work better.

After several months of making all of the necessary preparations, Dionisio's parents started their enterprise to begin their new life in La Costa. They bought a small two-story house one block away from La Tercera avenue and very close to La Principal. Dionisio grew up with the heat of the tropics, with the murmurs of the waves, and with a passionate distaste for any type of food coming from the guts of the ocean, which he considered appropriate to admire, but not as a source of beings marinated in its filthy waters to be serve as food.

The sea has a peculiar effect on humans: the mix of salt with heat creates a delicious seasoning, which makes people, even if they are poor or have had a terrible life, to be very happy and joyful. Dionisio lacked this seasoning. He was happy in his own way, but it was difficult for him to show it. When he was a kid, people would worry about him because he was too serious and they told his parents to take him places like the circus, the movies, or parks for him to have some fun and smile. Mr. and Mrs. Diosdado would take these comments seriously, and more often than not, they will take his son to try to have fun. Sometimes Dionisio would smile watching the silly and stupid things the clowns did, or laugh at a joke told in the movie he watched. Those were the moments that made Mr. and Mrs. Diosdado's souls rest a little.

"Do not forget our deal," The Death would say to Dionisio anytime She thought he was too happy.
"How can I forget when you constantly remind me of it?" Dionisio would answer, with a fading smile of someone that has seen something horrible.

Part 4

The large windows made the walls of the bridge that served as a connecting hallway between the two identical buildings. Dionisio enjoyed standing in the middle of the bridge looking through the window while eating an invariable ham and swiss cheese sandwich for lunch. From there, he could clearly see the immensity of the ocean, the ships floating at the distance, the warm mist hiding the horizon, and the dark gray clouds carrying storms towards the city. This was his small refuge to free himself from the day's burdens. He had finished college a couple of years back and with the aid of a professor that treated him as an exceptional student, he landed a job as a genetic analyst in a bioinformatics company. At the beginning, he ran assays to test for genetic defects, which he eventually improved, thereby proving himself as a valuable asset. He rose through the ranks and quickly became the scientist manager of the company's branch. With this promotion, his responsibilities increased and gradually became more demanding. He was in charge of making sure that every single assay was run according to protocol, that the results were clear and unambiguous, and that everything was done efficiently, practically, and economically. That is why he looked forward to his lunch, when for a brief period of time, he could enjoy religiously his ham and swiss cheese sandwich and lose himself in the immensity of the ocean.

"Hello," said the woman that had approached him.
He did not answer. He was focused on the bouncing lightings inside the clouds a few miles out at sea. He imagined the thunder, the rain falling hard on the ocean, and the fish enjoying the waves that come and go. 'Would the fish fry when lightning hits the ocean?' he would constantly ask himself.
"Hello," said again the woman, a bit louder.
Dionisio turned around to look at the woman who was interrupting his thoughts.
"Yes?" he answered, flustered.
"I just wanted to say hello. I often see you standing there eating your lunch when I cross the bridge, always looking at the ocean."
"That's correct," he answered, turning back to the window.
The clouds were rapidly approaching the shore. The wind increased and it was clear that the

afternoon was going to be stormy. Claudia saw the clouds in the distance and chills ran down her spine. She turned to look at Dionisio one more time. He ignored her. She turned around and walked towards her building. Dionisio followed her through the window's reflection. When she was no longer there, Dionisio instinctively lowered his head to look at the palm of his hand, where the skin foldings formed an "M": he followed the longest fold, the one that reaches the base of the hand, known by palm readers as the 'Line of Life'. His line bifurcated in the middle and reunited creating an oval resembling an eye. An eye that looked back at him. He recalled the first time that Magdalena read his fortune on his palm. He shook his head to come out of the brief trance and looked up to come back to his thoughts in the horizon once more.

Part 5

Claudia lived all her childhood in Salamanca. Her grandfather, her father's father, bought a piece of land outside of the city, and with a lot of work and effort, he built five small houses; one for each of his children and their families. Claudia grew up in that small community, always being taken care of by her parents or any other of her relatives. She was happy and content. However, the Alicante family was shaken by a couple of events that changed Claudia's life forever. One Ash Wednesday the weather turned crazy. In the morning the sun came out for a couple of hours, warming the city and then hiding itself behind a massive cold front. Darkness promptly covered the city by midday. The lightning came first, then the thunder. One of those lightnings directly hit the antenna of Claudia's dad car at the exact moment he opened the door to get in. The volts travelled

unstopped from the antenna to the door handle and to
Mr. Alicante's heart. He died immediately and without
pain. His body smelled like cooked muscle. Three
hours after this incident, the rain had increased and
looked like a gray curtain unfolding from the sky. The
streets flooded with fast moving creeks full of trash,
leaves, and tree branches, which reached the sewers
in an unorganized clutter, clogging them. The
firefighters were working hard under the rain trying to
reduce the flooding. They removed the covers of the
manholes to let the water drain better, but the amount
of the liquid was more than what the city could hold.
Mrs. Alicante, grocery shopping and unaware of the
death of her husband a few hours ago, took refuge
under a store's awning. She grew restless waiting and
decided to head back home. She knew she was going
to get drenched, but resigned herself to that destiny.
She started walking the best she could under the rain,
immersed knee-deep in the flood. When she crossed
the street, she did not see under the dark waters the
missing manhole that opened its mouth to swallow
her completely in one big gulp. In one short instant,
Mrs. Alicante disappeared without anyone noticing it.
Her purple swollen body was found two days later
floating at the end of the main city drain, but not
alone: there were five other bodies accompanying
her.

Part 6

A great void entered Claudia's life and soul.
Her parents' death followed her all the days of her
long life. She missed them dearly. Her only comfort
was to see them in dreams where she could talk to
them, play with them, laugh with them. Many times,
she would cry inside herself, she wanted to feel them,

see them. She hated thunderstorms and had an irrational fear of them: the noise of the rain hitting the roof of the house or the roof of the car invoked a terrible fear. She would become paralyzed with thunder and lightning, losing her speech and her self-control. This fear would fill the void left by her parents.

Claudia was well taken care of by the rest of the Alicante family, especially her grandparents, who claimed her as their own child. But their care was overwhelming and exaggerated. Claudia felt asphyxiated and enclosed in a caring bubble. She was forbidden to go out with friends to the movies or parties; staying the night at friends' houses was inconceivable. Claudia would close herself to the world and open herself to a journal where she would write her thoughts and frustrations. Sometimes Claudia would think about her death, about how her family would repent about isolating her from the world, she could even hear her grandmother cry and scream "I should have let her be herself." These thoughts were all expressed on her journal. Claudia loved her family but she never wrote that feeling down.

School was an oasis for her, a place where she could breathe without feeling observed or oppressed. She was fortunate to be very intelligent, which helped her to be accepted in one of the most prestigious private schools in the city. When alive, her parents were able to afford the school's tuition with what Mr. Alicante made. But after that expense, there was little left over for other things. When they died during the Ash Wednesday storm, the school board met and decided to provide Claudia with a full scholarship, as long as she maintained an A average. That was not too difficult for her.

Part 7

The girl was tall and blond, and Dionisio thought she was an angel. Her skin was white, may be a little too much, hugging her slender teenager figure. Her legs were long like pipes hanging from her body. She was not extremely beautiful, but she was different: a white mole in the middle of a brown-skin monotony. All the boys liked her and paid a lot of attention to her, the difference with Dionisio is that she directly and firmly stabbed his weak heart.

She was not the first girl that drew Dionisio's eyes and attention. When he was in elementary school, barely 9 years old, a short, sweet girl with a baby face itched his curiosity. Dionisio did not know how to approach or talk to her, and he would just be happy watching her from the distance during recess or being mesmerized by her during classes. Her name was Luna. During those days, the only friend that the skinny and shy Dionisio had was Miguel, a simple and common kid that could get lost in a crowd and nobody would look after him. Miguel had very few skills, but he knew how to engage in a conversation and extract all the juicy gossipy details. Dionisio enjoyed Miguel's company, he would talk and play with him. One day out of the blue, Dionisio blurted out that he liked Luna and made Miguel pinky swear that he would not tell anyone about it. He also mentioned that he did not know how to talk to her. Miguel gave him absolutely no advice, for the simple reason that he did not know anything about how to approach girls. However, Miguel burned in his mind every single word Dionisio told him with the sole purpose of telling verbatim this sweet information to any willing ear. Forget the pinky swear, he said to himself. Miguel passed Dionisio's love to Luna to anyone who would listen, mostly all students and even some faculty. Luna heard it as well, but she took it lightly and thought that it was nice to have an admirer. The news also landed in the ears of a small, good-for-nothing gang of 10-year-olds, which decided to take Dionisio's inaction into their own hands. One ordinary day, they surrounded both Dionisio and Luna, intimidated them a little, then took them to an empty classroom. There, they twisted their arms behind their backs, pushed them together close and made them kiss each other forcefully. Luna was completely in shocked and frankly scared to death. Dionisio, on the other hand, secretly enjoyed that bodily interaction until the moment that one of the kids asked him if he was getting hard. Dionisio, which had become hard at the first moment he touched Luna's lips, turned red and shame ran through his small body. So much was his shame that he fought hard to free himself. He did, and he ran; he ran so fast and as far as he could possibly go. From that moment, in his kid's mind, all girls stopped existing and Dionisio decided to just study and forget the world.

"I think that is the reason you are so horny all the time," said Claudia with a big smile on her face.
"I think so too." answered Dionisio.

Ena was the name of the tall, blond, skinny legged girl. Middle school could be cruel to many, the time when girls would develop faster than most of the boys. Dionisio was short and thin, truly just a piece of an incomplete boy, and he looked at Ena as an Amazonian goddess that was at least a foot taller than him. The first time Dionisio saw Ena was at the beginning of the year and it took only that time for him to become severely injured by her looks. At that moment, Ena removed Dionisio's repulsion against girls that Luna had instilled on him. During the first days of classes, Dionisio would look at Ena and he would imagine their lives developing together, going to the movies as a couple, talking to her about everything and nothing, getting married, having four or five beautiful kids and living a fairy tale life that his very young mind imagined. Dionisio thought that he had found the girl of his life, the woman that one day he would introduce to his parents and they would smile and be proud of his perfect choice. He was still a kid, but he knew his life was happily set. The only detail missing, which was sort of the most important, was to find the courage to approach Ena, introduce himself, and let his plans turn into reality.

Dionisio had to wait a couple of months to speak his first words to Ena. During an ordinary recess, Dionisio was playing tag, when he suddenly skidded, lost control of himself and ended up crashing against Ena. Both bounced together for a few feet. Ena immediately stood up and blurted out a rosary of curses towards the stupid piece of a boy that knocked her down. Dionisio tried to interrupt her with apologies that never reached Ena's ears. Despite the shame he endured that moment, Dionisio had one of the best days of his short life. When he got home he could not stop thinking about the incident, in his mind he relived, with more fantasy than certainty, the moment that his body collided with hers, and the conversation (that never was one) that ensued.

Dionisio fell asleep thinking about the next day's conversation he was planning to have with her. According to his plan, he would come to her to apologize one more time, and after that he would tell her a great joke he had just thought of: a polar bear cub asked his polar bear mom whether he indeed was a polar bear, to which the mom answered yes. The polar bear cub would repeat the same question many times until the mom, growing impatiently, asked him, 'why are you asking me if you are a polar bear?'; the cub answered, 'well, I do not know about you, but I am freezing!' A foolproof joke that would make Ena forget all about the incident, but most importantly, would open the opportunity to have a second interaction with her, and for her to realize that Dionisio was the man, or rather the boy, she needed.

The next day, a Wednesday, Dionisio woke up earlier than usual, he dressed and had a quick breakfast. He hurried his dad to take him to school as fast as possible. Once in school, Dionisio waited impatiently, biting his nails, for Ena to enter the classroom. The first hour went by with no signs of Ena around. Dionisio thought and convinced himself that Ena was running obviously late. After the second hour passed while listening to a teacher that said unintelligible words that Dionisio never understood because his mind was somewhere else, Dionisio thought that Ena was so upset with him that she decided not to go to school, a thought that scratched Dionisio's mind like nails on a chalkboard. He suddenly realized his plans were about to crash down. When the school day ended, without hope, Dionisio heard from one of Ena's friends that she missed school because she went on vacation with her family, and that she would not come back until the following Monday. Dionisio's stomach turned when he thought about the time distance ahead of him, which was only 5 days away, but for him was an eternity. And indeed, it was.

Monday came slowly, finding Dionisio restless and eager to get to school. He memorized and repeated constantly in his mind the words he would use. He even knew, with almost one hundred percent certainty, the words that Ena would use to respond to him. Everything was going according to plan, at least in his young boy's mind. Ena entered the classroom while talking to a friend, as usual; but for Dionisio, her entrance was as if a queen had stepped in royally into a dance hall. Dionisio looked at her like a fool, felt his weak heart go into overdrive, his hands started to sweat and his stomach was in knots. He tried to get close to her, but the teacher came into the classroom and he had no other option but to wait for recess. Once the bell rang, Dionisio dashed to the restroom because his nerves had turned liquid. Rested, Dionisio wrapped himself in courage and searched for the woman of his life, which he found very quickly because she was not far away, talking to a group of friends. Dionisio breathed deeply, walked over to Ena and with a shaky and boyish voice blurted a sentence that sounded more like grunts. Ena looked at him and asked him what in the world he was saying. Dionisio, a bit calmer explained to her the incident and wanted to apologize to her. She was barely paying attention and said nothing. Dionisio was taken aback because a 'no response' was not the answer he had expected. As a survival instinct, Dionisio started telling the polar bear joke, but the nerves made the joke completely incoherent. Ena laughed, not at the joke, that at that moment was just a mixed of scrambled words, but at him. She laughed maliciously. Shame inundated Dionisio's little body, he lowered his head and left with tear-flooded eyes.

"What a bitch of a girl that Ena was! I am sorry!" Claudia said as she tenderly squeezed Dionisio's arm.

"Yes, she was."

During the end of the year break, Dionisio's parents took him to a Christmas show. Although the show was a complete disaster, Dionisio will remember that day because it was the day he befriended Magdalena, a girl that Dionisio never realized until that moment, that she was a classmate of his. Magdalena wore big, round, think glasses, and braces on her teeth. Magdalena liked to talk, a lot. She came to Dionisio and introduced herself to him (she knew he had no idea who she was, despite being together in the same class). Their conversation was short. When classes resumed, Magdalena took the initiative to strike up conversations with her new friend. She would look for him during recess, in classes, and when they finished for the day. She was not shy. She liked hugging him, messed with his hair, pinched him and sometimes she would kiss Dionisio on the cheek, something he found uncomfortable. He did not mind Magdalena's company or the physical contact, except for the kisses. On the contrary, he liked being around her and realized that he could talk to her about anything. They conversed about classes, teachers and the nicknames they would use to describe them, TV shows, they would make stories, and sometimes they would talk about the end of the world or the anti-Christ appearance somewhere in La Costa.

"I am going to read your palm," said an excited Magdalena
"Why?"

"To see your future."

"I don't believe in those things."

"You believe in the anti-Christ. Please, let me do it."

Reluctantly, Dionisio extended his left hand. She studied it as if reading a historical document. She looked professional.

"You have a very peculiar Life Line," said Magdalena, pointing at his fold, "it looks like it forms a little oval. I have never seen something like this."

It was also Dionisio's first realization of his palm folding.

"What does that mean?" he asked, a bit worried.

"I don't know, but I know it's important." Magdalena diagnosed.

"What do you mean important?"

"I do not know, but it is."

"How do you know it's important if you don't know what it means?"

"Because you are the only person that I have seen with something like that."

One day during recess, Dionisio and Magdalena played pretending to touch something invisible with their hands, like a wall. Both laughed like crazy. While doing this, a small crowd of classmates made a circle around them trying to figure out what the two of them were doing. Dionisio and Magdalena ignored the crowd until Ena, with a very sweet voice, asked Dionisio what they were doing. He stopped immediately and turned to face her. Dionisio could not say a word but Magdalena came immediately to his rescue.

"We are touching the Great Wall of China," she said nonchalantly.

"What do you mean?" Ena replied.

Dioniso finally came out of his silence and explained:

"The air particles touch each other, and these touch the ground, and the ground touches the center of the earth, and the center of the earth touches the ground beneath the Great Wall of China. And when we touch the air particles we are touching the Great Wall of China."

It was hard to tell who was more surprised, Ena to hear that interesting but rather stupid explanation, or Dionisio, who had just had a conversation with her without becoming nervous or shy. Ena then joined them and started pretending that she was touching a big wall. Other classmates followed her cue.

The silly Great Wall of China game brought Ena closer to Dionisio and Magdalena. She was surprised of the conversations these two had. They were really interesting but also funny and she could not stop laughing. She tried whenever she could to participate with a tale or story she considered somewhat funny. Dionisio and Magdalena accepted her stories with a good amount of grace. Dionisio, Magdalena, and Ena became a trio of friends that for a season were inseparable. To Dionisio, this was both a blessing and a curse: on one hand, he spent immeasurable minutes beside Ena, but on the other, he realized that he lacked the courage to tell her about the great love he had for her as well as his awesome plans he had delineated with exquisite detail for both of their lives. One real positive thing that came out of these times was that Dionisio was so busy at school and with his two friends that he forgot that The Death was constantly around him.

Ena was not a fool, she knew well that Dionisio was after her. It was obvious. Dionisio tried to be as close to her as possible, he would rub his hand against her hands or arms as if it were by accident, or he would pretend to remove some lint or hair from her shoulder. Ena barely tolerated his behavior and she would let him know with not very kind facial expressions that Dionisio noticed but ignored. But Ena liked his attention and did not say a word about the unexpected physical touch.

Pablo was a boy that, contrary to most other boys in school, was tall and full of well-defined muscles for a kid his age. He liked to play soccer, was very good at it, and constantly bragged about his skills when pickup games started during recess. Pablo had only one defect: his nose looked like a toucan beak. Despite this horny defect, Pablo was one of the most coveted kids in school, especially by Ena and Magdalena, who preferred to ignore the nose and focus on his other attributes. Some girls even commented that that was the reason bed pillows were invented, a saying that probably a few of them understood. Pablo was every other boy's envy. One Monday in March, while they were waiting for the teacher to arrive, Dionisio, Magdalena, and Ena were talking about the weekend happenings. Dionisio mentioned that he spent Sunday watching soccer on TV, to what Ena followed by saying that Pablo, one day, would become one of the best soccer players in the country. Dionisio responded by saying that the toucan would never become a professional player. Ena and Magdalena looked at each other full of fury and during the entirety of that day did not talk anymore to him. He did not care.

Ena admired Pablo and it was very hard for her to forget and forgive the way Dionisio talked about him. That same day, while walking back home from school, she reached the conclusion that just for spite, she would make Pablo fall in love with her. For sure, this action would show Dionisio that even someone with a horrible nose could be her boyfriend, but never him. That same day, Dionisio, without knowing it, lost every single possibility for his plans to become reality. Ena stopped being a real friend to him.

The following days were of total confusion for both Dionisio and Magdalena because the only thing Ena was interested in doing was pursuing Pablo every single possible moment. She spent very little time with them, and when she did, she was absorbed in her thoughts. Dionisio and Magdalena asked themselves why Ena was behaving like that, but were not able to answer their questions. Finally, they decided to directly ask her. Ena, without a sign of hesitation, told them that she was interested in making new friends.

Pablo never realized that Ena was using him as a vendetta against Dionisio, as a punishment for insulting him. The poor logic of Ena's argument seemed not to bother her. Ena would sit on Pablo's muscular legs and she would let Pablo rub her skinny ones. They would kiss with scandalous kisses, always Ena trying to avoid Pablo's enormous protuberance. And they would talk about their great love they had for each other any chance they had. This behavior increased when Dionisio was close by. The rest of the school looked at them as the most magical couple, they would whisper that they were made for each other, that their kids would be the most beautiful kids in the country as long as they inherited mom's nose. A fairy tale turned into reality.

While everybody, including Magdalena that had forgiven Ena as if nothing had happened, admired and were joyful about the new couple, Dionisio fell like the world was crumbling around him and that his sentimental future was collapsing in front of his nose, ironically, because of a kid with a huge nose. His good grades disappeared because he was unable to concentrate. On top of that, his weak heart started to bother him and at least a couple of times his parents had to take him to the hospital where he spent a few days. Some classmates visited him, including Ena and Pablo, while The Death, standing always in the corner of the hospital room, watched attentively. He begged Her to take him right there, but She reminded him of Her promise.

And then, maybe a month after the fairy tale couple made its appearance, the unexpected happened: Pablo announced to Ena and his friends that his parents had decided to move to the north of the country and that this would happen in about two weeks. Ena collapsed with the news, especially because by that time she had truly fallen in love with him. She took her refuge in Dionisio who welcome her back into his life with open arms. He was walking on clouds. Pablo left La Costa and became a mediocre professional soccer player, lasting only two seasons. Years later, on an April morning, his body was found hung from a soccer goal post. His huge purple nose pointing down at the green grass.

The week after Pablo's departure was magical for Dionisio. He had an inconsolable and fragile Ena in his arms, which he would caress and kiss on her cheeks or hair to help her cope with her dire situation, or at least that is what he would tell her. Dionisio thought that his plan, their plan, had taken on a new life. However, as fast as Pablo left, Pedro arrived. Pedro was not in the same classes as Dionisio, Magdalena, and Ena, but he was in the same grade. Pedro was not the most handsome boy in the school, but he had charisma. Like the rest of the school boys, Pedro was very attracted to Ena but he knew that while Pablo was around, he had zero chances with her; however, once Pablo was out of the picture, he planned and made his move fast. Two weeks later, after Pablo left town, Pedro stood in front of Ena, Dionisio, and Magdalena during recess and asked Ena if he could talk to her. The three of them were surprised, especially because Pedro was not someone they would talk to, but they knew who he was. Pedro and Ena walked a few yards away enough for them not to be overheard by Dionisio and Magdalena. They talked for about five minutes ending with Ena hugging Pedro's neck and with a passionate kiss that left Dionisio and Magdalena with their mouths hanging.

Dionisio's misfortune, as misfortunes tend to do, came at the worst of times. Ena fell in love with Pedro; something that looked very easy for her to do. She would not stop talking about him, how good he was with her, that Pablo was not even the shadow of him, and that for sure she had found the man, or boy, of her life. Pedro, in a smart move, tried to befriend Dionisio and Magdalena. He tried to be with them as much as he could, thinking that being close to Ena's friends was a great strategy. The worst part for Dionisio was that Pedro was a wonderful and kind boy, not only with Ena, but with the three of them. He had an enchanting and persuasive voice that could convince anyone to do anything. Pedro was a leader, and despite that he had plucked Ena away from him, Dionisio admired him.

Pedro and Dionisio became good friends. The four of them would get together during recess, Pedro would hug Ena and talk to them about the most relevant thing of the day. Pedro did not like to listen to himself talk, but the three of them preferred more to listen than to provide something to the conversation. Pedro lived in the same direction as Dionisio, close to La Tercera, and sometimes they waited for each other at the end of the day to walk together. They would kick stones, count cars, and talk about boy things as they walked along La Principal. Sometimes Pedro would mention Ena and how adorable and beautiful she was. Dionisio would just nod as envy and sadness covered his weak heart.

"Do you think Ena would like a red rose as a present for the second week of being a couple?" asked Pedro, full of happiness as if he were the one receiving the rose.

"She would love it." answered Dionisio, with little enthusiasm.

"Would you do me a favor?" asked Pedro after a small silence.

"Sure."

"I want the rose to be a surprise, would you give it to her from my part?"

Dionisio hesitated, but then answered that he would do it. Two days later, Dionisio arrived to school with a huge red rose and a small card that drew everybody's attention, which included one or two kids asking, not in a nice way, if the flower was for his 'girlfriend'. Dionisio just shook his head. When Ena entered the classroom, Dionisio, as if he were a dead man walking, moved towards her and gave her the presents while she looked at him very suspiciously. Ena opened the card hesitantly, but when she read it she screamed sharply and jumped up and down a few times. She even hugged Dionisio, unintentionally. He just simply lowered his head.

"You became the messenger," said Claudia.
"Yes. I thought about distancing myself from Ena and Pedro, but I couldn't. At that moment, I believed that having her close to me was better than not having her at all."
Claudia looked at him pitifully, hugged him, and kissed him with a good wet kiss on the neck.

For Magdalena's 12th birthday, she organized a small party with her best friends. Of the thirty people she invited, only ten went, including Dionisio, Ena, and Pedro. They danced a little, drank punch, told stupid jokes, and ate a vanilla cake that had an incredible amount of very sweet icing. At the end of the party, they played Truth or Dare. When most of the kids had answered a question or done something silly, it was Dionisio's turn. Ernesto, a boy from the same classroom as Dionisio, asked him directly and intentionally who was the love of his life. Dionisio shook his head to let Ernesto know that he was not going to answer that question. But the peer pressure was intense and he had no other option but to answer it. He could have lied, but he answered with such clarity as if his life depended on it.

"Ena. She is the love of my life and there will be no other woman that would touch my heart as she has done."

The room went silent. Awkward. Ena and Pedro looked at each other and then looked angrily at Dionisio. He was red as an apple.

Ena did not tolerate what Dionisio had said about her being the love of his life. He knew that she and Pedro were very happy. That is something a friend should not say, even if it were true. She got sick, nauseated at the idea of that little piece of a boy being in love with her. Yes, she knew he liked her, but being in love was a different thing. Pedro thought that what Dionisio said was wrong. He did not think beyond that, and stopped talking to him. Magdalena was the only one that stayed with him. Dionisio tried to fix things with Ena and Pedro, but it was useless: an invisible wall grew overnight between their friendship and never came down.

Dionisio spent the last two years of middle school trying to avoid Ena and Pedro, and at the same time, he endured the idea that now it was impossible for Ena to be with him. And at the very end of middle school, when most kids were looking forward to moving to different high schools and beginning a new adventure, Ena stabbed Dionisio's heart for the last time. Dionisio, with a lot of effort and hesitation, approached her without caring that she was surrounded by many friends including Pedro. He stood in front of her trying to avoid her scrutinizing gaze. And he undressed his heart in front of her.

"This could very well be the last time that we see each other and I want to tell you that you are the most beautiful girl I have ever met and that I would like to kiss you and hug at least once before we move to a different school." recited Dionisio, without a pause, it was obvious he had memorized well what he wanted to say.

"Go and fuck yourself," barked Ena, while a cold and calculated smile painted her face.

Everyone laughed at that piece of a boy that lowered his head, his face red of shame and frustration, and with nascent tears in his eyes. His soul was humiliated. He got out of there as fast as possible and ran, exited the school, and found refuge under the shade of an enormous mango tree. For everybody else, it was a beautiful sunny day, a day that was planned to be spent at the beach, all but Dionisio. He sat under the mango tree and cried forever. In his solitude, he felt his heart beat at an irregular pace.

The Death could be terrible, but cruelty is not at Her core. The Death saw his sadness. She wanted to care for him, help him. She left him alone for a few years to let his weak heart rest. For now, he had had enough.

Part 8

"What do you look at, through the window?"
"The ocean."
"But you look at it very intensely, what do you see in it?"

Dionisio felt chased with the nonstop questions that this woman constantly asked him. He avoided looking at her face.

"A lot of things, I don't know, its color, immensity, the rhythm of the waves," he answered, bothered.

"Claudia Alicante." she said, as if announcing someone important.

"Pardon?"

"My name is Claudia Alicante and I worked in tower B. I just moved to La Costa a few weeks ago. I love the ocean, the beach, the heat, the sun constantly touching my face, oh, and the smell of salt coming from the sea!"
A pause. Dionisio was terrified of how fast that woman spoke.

"Good."

He hesitated, but then decided to continue with this conversation. This was not the first time this woman, or Claudia Alicante as she called herself, interrupted his lunch. Maybe, he thought, if he talked to her for a little while, she would leave him alone.

"Where are you moving from?" he asked, pretending to be interested.

"From Salamanca."

"Oh! I was born there."

"Me too!"

Dionisio thought carefully for a second.

"I think I have met you before. You seem familiar."

"Maybe in Salamanca?"

"No, I have not been there since the time I moved, and that was when I was very little. It doesn't matter, I need to finish my sandwich. It was nice talking to you."

He turned facing the window to look once more at the ocean. In the glass reflection, he saw Claudia standing behind him, smiling at him. He smiled back and she left.

The sea was calm. Seagulls flew in tranquility and Dionisio felt peace, a feeling he had not experienced in a long time. He smiled again, he saw his smile reflected in the window. He finished his lunch and left without noticing that over the ocean, close to the seagulls, The Death was floating.

Claudia and Dionisio

Part 1

What is this jerk telling me? Claudia asked herself.

"I am serious. You and I have the chance to attract each other and fall in love. When this happens, we need to talk about it, so we can avoid it." said Dionisio in a very casual way.

"Avoid what?" she would rather keep looking at the reports she needed to read than to listen to this man's nonsense.

"Avoid the mutual attraction."

Claudia decided not to continue. But it was true, from the moment she met Dionisio, she noticed something familiar with this man, a closeness.

Part 2

When Claudia reached puberty, her body did not help her when. Her legs and arms were very long, her hands and feet looked masculine, her teeth lost all orientation and grew anyway they wanted demanding the use of braces. She hated them. Acne waited no time to mercilessly invade her face so much that multiple layers of makeup could not conceal it. She lost that battle. The only two things that comforted her was her ass, round and firm, like her mom's, and her growing breasts. She was amazed at the speed they grew but as a fast as they increased in size, they stopped: they were just a pair of lemons. Claudia did everything possible to resuscitate their growth: lotions, oils, exercises that girls' magazines promised to be one hundred percent guaranteed. Nothing worked.

On top of all her body issues, Claudia's period started. She was only ten years old and the first period came with spells of dizziness, sciatic pain, migraines, and a scary gorilla-like temper. Her grandparents tried to not get too close when the blood was flowing. That was not a bad thing for Claudia that loved to be alone. Sometimes she even told her family she was on her period, just to avoid conversations with them.

The change in hormone flow caused even more issues. At a very early age she would feel heat waves coming from her lower abdomen rush upwards. She would tremble in her insides. She did not know what was happening to her; at the beginning, she thought she was sick. Finally, she told her grandmother about these heat waves, and she just told Claudia that those were women's things and that when one of the waves would come she should think about all the famine children in the world. Claudia did not understand her grandmother's advice, but decided to follow it. The heat, as she called it, arrived suddenly and could stay with her for a few days. When this would happen, Claudia would make every effort to concentrate herself in starving kids. In her imagination, she would feed them with rice with meat and orange juice. When the heat was even more intense, Claudia would forget the rice and the meat and she would concentrate only in the orange juice; she could taste and smell it, and she would tell the starving kids that the juice was delicious. Sometimes the kids would disappear from her mind leaving her alone with the juice aroma, the oranges aroma. Then her imagination would take her to an orange tree orchard, and she would fly above it as if she were a spirt. She would see the trees and the branches with intense green leaves filling everything, the scent of oranges flooding the region, flooding every pore of her body. Claudia would smell the scent, she would enjoy it while flying above the infinite orange tree orchard. The heat would grow and travel rapidly throughout her body, she would sweat and her legs would start to tremble. Breathing would be difficult. Claudia would fly closer to the trees, she would touch them and take a big juicy orange from a branch. She would carefully take it with her hand, as if it were a precious treasure. She would caress it, putting the orange skin closer to hers. Then she would squeeze the fruit, the heat would increase, one more squeeze and the juice would explode out promiscuously from the tiny holes in the orange peel. After the adventure, Claudia would end up exhausted but happy because she was able to tame the heat.

Part 3

"Dionisio, do you remember the first conversation we had?"

"The first one? Sure, when you would bother me in the bridge while I was trying to have my lunch in peace."

"Those were not conversations, you were just a jerk, only answering with yes, no, or maybe."

Part 4

Claudia cruised through middle school easily. Courses were not a challenge for her and sometimes they were just boring. She would spend long mornings writing in her notebooks, not about the words that came out as rosaries from the teachers' mouths flooding the classroom, but about small circular stories with no end; stories that portrayed her feelings about being trapped in a place or body that was not hers. The stories made her travel to impossible places where she could be free of all bondage tying her down to the life given to her. Sometimes her stories would take her to the familiar orange tree orchards; she would fly above the trees' canopies enjoying the orange scent. She would grab an orange to squeeze the juice out of it. And the heat would be summoned, or maybe it had been already there, she couldn't tell. She would close her eyes; the words of the teacher would fade away with the orange scent; her legs tightly crossed. She would start to tremble while the heat waves would travel throughout her body, she would tighten her lips and the same time her hand would squeeze the orange, and when the juice would be flowing on her hands, she would wake up from her travel, look at her notes, her classmates, her teacher, all of them oblivious to what she had just experienced. Claudia would smile with satisfaction. Back home, she would again read her stories, but they did not have the same effect - simple phrases with little meaning, already read and lacking novelty.

Claudia had no interest in boys, she thought that they were very immature and not very entertaining. She thought like that due to the fact that all the other girls, that were developing much faster than her and had more adequate proportions, were monopolizing the boys' attention. Of course, Claudia had some envy about those girls; she felt herself to be not very attractive. Her grandparents, with the wisdom accumulated throughout the years, knew that it was the season for Claudia to start paying attention to boys, or vice versa, but they also knew that she was still developing and that could be a problem to her self-esteem. Thus, to help her, they subtly mentioned to her one Saturday morning that the day will come when her body will finish developing and it would give rise to a beautiful woman. Claudia immediately asked them with a not very friendly tone, '*are you telling me that I am ugly now but will later be beautiful?*' At that point, the grandparents' wisdom was nowhere to be seen, and they ended up stumbling, making excuses, and sometimes preaching stories of people Claudia had never met.

Despite her feelings, which were accentuated by her grandparents' comments, there was a first spark of love that came from a boy named Joaquín Villagrán, a tiny and insignificant boy that was as tall as Claudia's chin. He wore glasses, had more freckles than clear skin, was extremely introverted, and liked to silently follow her. He would look at her from the distance and sometimes he would leave her small anonymous and corny notes in her bag-pack. Claudia noticed all that Joaquín was doing because he was not very careful and on more than one occasion she turned her head to purposely lock her eyes with his, and made him turn around. Claudia loved these types of interactions, but Joaquín did not stir up the butterflies inside her.

On one November day, when the city had cooled down and the days were a bit shorter, Claudia was walking back home, somewhat self-absorbed in her own thoughts, when she suddenly noticed a presence, as if someone were following her. She did not turn around immediately, but in her periphery, she could see that it was the conspicuous Joaquín. She walked a few steps more to make sure that it really was him following her. When she was completely sure, she turned around fast, and without intention, startled the poor boy that, in an attempt to flee, also turned around quickly, but not completely, and started running. He never saw the huge oak tree trunk that was at the edge of the sidewalk. Glasses, freckles, and the rest of Joaquín were smeared on the tree. After a few moments, Joaquín's body peeled off of the tree and finished collapsed at the oak's foot. Claudia quickly ran to help him. She lifted him up and noticed that his face was full of purple scratches, some of them bleeding. She took a small handkerchief from her bag and carefully cleaned him. Joaquín did not lose consciousness, but he could not clearly see because his glasses were destroyed. His head was spinning. He felt arms hugging him and hands cleaning his wounds, but did not know it was Claudia until the pain decreased and he could focus his sight. He was in her arms. He got scared again and tried to escape, but Claudia stopped him.

"You are so dumb, Joaquín!" said Claudia, a bit entertained, "Why do you keep on following me?"

Joaquín looked at her but did not answer. His body started trembling.

"My goodness Joaquín, you are truly a case! I am going to take you to your home, my grandparents are not going to like the idea, but they will understand that it was an emergency."

Claudia walked with him to his house. She knocked and a small, thin woman opened the door. The woman put her hands up to her mouth when she saw Joaquín's condition and promptly started assisting him.

"My dear little boy! What happened to you? Did somebody hit you at school? Was it that good-for-nothing Marco? Tell me now and I will go to his house to tell his mother what kind of a beast her son is!"

When Joaquín did not answer, maybe because of fear or pain, and his mom was ready to execute a crusade against Marco, Claudia decided to intervene.

"No ma'am, it was not like that."

Joaquín's mom realized at that moment that his son was not alone, but in the company of and physically supported by that girl talking to her now.

"What?" the mom answered, surprised.

"What I mean to say is that no one attacked Joaquín. He crashed against a tree when he was running."

The mom looked at Claudia with inquisitive and non-friendly eyes.

"How in the world is it that my son crashed against a tree, that is ridiculous!"

"Well, he didn't see it, he was distracted."

"What could have distracted him in such a way? That is absurd!"
Claudia realized the conversation was going to lead to an uncomfortable situation, and against her principles, she lied.

"Apparently a dog came out from nowhere trying to attack him and that distracted Joaquín."

The mom turned to look at Joaquín to interrogate him one more time.

"Was it the useless Pinto? That ungrateful beast of an animal that belongs to the old lady? Tell me and I will march there right now to yell in her face. It's time that someone put that horrible monster to sleep for a long, long time."

Joaquín, that until that moment was only listening to the conversation between his vengeful mother and Claudia, interrupted.

"No mom, it wasn't Pinto…it was a stray dog."

The mother was not convinced and wanted to avenge her son in any way possible. She ran into the house to get some gauze and alcohol. Rather confused, Claudia stood close to Joaquín, which was now sitting close to the door.

"Thank you, for not telling my mom the real reason."

"Don't mention it. But you have to be less stupid and maybe take more risks. If you want to talk to me, just do it. Don't hide. Alright, I'm leaving because my grandparents for sure are going to be worrying about me by now."

Without hesitation, Claudia crouched beside him to hug him and give him a nice kiss on his cheeks full of scratches. Joaquín came to life. He watched her leave, still enjoying the hug and the kiss, until the mom came to clean Joaquín's wounds right there at the entrance of the house, and to continue harassing him over the details of the stray monster that attacked her son. She was ready to call the closest dog pound with euthanizing facilities.

Joaquín's behavior changed radically the next day after the tree crash. He would get together with Claudia during recess and talk to her about anything that came to his mind. Claudia was fascinated with the new Joaquín. In reality, Joaquín was pretty smart; he spoke eloquently and his stories were interesting and entertaining. Most of those stories seemed as if he had made them up. Many years later, Claudia would listen to Dionisio's unending stories and Joaquín would come to her mind, but with the enormous difference that Claudia listened to Dionisio's stories as if they were part of her memory.

Joaquín was small, but a true rascal. In one of those occasions in which the two of them would sit to talk, he decided to rest his hand, without worries, on Claudia's legs that were only covered above the knees by her skirt. Claudia felt the warmth of that small hand that softly rubbed her, but she did not react. She was thunderstruck, enjoying for a few moments that touch. She lowered her sight and saw that his hand was ascending at a slow but determined pace. She then realized what was happening and slapped without mercy Joaquín's cheek. His new glasses, because the old pair were useless after the tree incident, flew a few yards away from him.

"Joaquín, what is wrong with you? Those are my legs!"

"I know," said Joaquín, reddened because of the slap, "but they are beautiful."
Claudia did not answer. She stood up to pick the glasses and put them on Joaquín. When she did, she kissed him on the red cheek. Joaquín became as red as a tomato and lowered his sight.

"Don't be stupid, Joaquín, you can talk to me, be my friend, we can spend time together, but never ever touch my legs again. Do you understand?"
Joaquín had no other option than to nod in agreement.

His thoughts were restless. He saw those well-formed legs hanging from the miniskirt and immediately the image of them was burned in his mind. He talked with her and subtly, he would look at her legs. Temptation grew and the images of him caressing those legs increased. She was driving and was paying close attention to the road. He decided to act, and casually extended his hand to touch her. It was a brief exploratory touch. She did not respond, the chat continued. Dionisio wanted to try his luck one more time, he waited a few minutes and then put his hand closer to his target. In this second attempt, he rested his hand as if Claudia's legs were the place his hand belonged to, and gently moved it up and down a couple of times. Contact lasted a few seconds. Claudia turned to look at him, unbothered, continuing the chat. From that moment on, Claudia had granted Dionisio the right to touch her legs at will. She was never bothered and thought that was the least she could do for that man. She was not fooling herself, she enjoyed his touch, a way to confirm that he would belong to her forever. She was not mistaken.

Claudia fell in love with Joaquín. That little boy reached her heart. He fulfilled his word and never touched Claudia's leg or any other part without her consent. Claudia would reward him with little kisses on the cheeks; she enjoyed how Joaquín would adore them. On his birthday, Claudia kissed him on the lips; that was the best present he had ever received in his life. Claudia's grandparents did not know about the kids' relationship and she made Joaquín promise not to call her at home, and to take any measure for them not to find out about their relationship. Joaquín agreed to everything she asked because he was very happy. Claudia enjoyed and loved his company until Joaquín's parents broke the news that they were moving to another city. One afternoon, hiding in the middle of a park, both kids cried their goodbyes, they kissed as children do and Claudia place his hand on her leg.

Years later, before Claudia moved to La Costa, a phone call interrupted her chores. Joaquín's grave voice was on the other side. Both were surprised to hear each other again. They exchanged the basic personal details of their recent lives and agreed to meet for coffee. They were very happy to see each other again. They hugged and talked for a long time. The night fell upon them and Joaquín ominously said goodbye to Claudia. She never knew it, but Joaquín died a few weeks after their reunion. Rumors ran than Joaquín had successfully attempted suicide, but the details were sketchy and a suicide was questionable: death by cutting his legs' arteries.

"I can't believe Joaquín did not propose to do something when you met him." Dionisio said.
"Not all men are like you! He is a good person and was a good boy, he respected me."
"Sure, respect, rubbing your legs,"
"It was only once!"
"Maybe he was gay and he was jealous of your gorgeous legs: he wanted those legs for his body!" Dionisio laughed loudly
"You are an ass."

Part 5

Dionisio's parents allowed him to be independent; every now and then they would give him some piece of advice or a warning, but most of the time they let him deal with life by himself. They knew his cardiac condition could take his life away at an early age and they wanted Dionisio to enjoy his life on his own terms. Dionisio knew from a very early age that his heart was not like everybody else's hearts; he knew he had health issues and needed to go to the doctor at least twice a year for a checkup. Doctors never found an adequate reason for his condition, and they as well as his parents were perplexed about his situation. Most of the time his heart beat correctly, but sometimes it would beat out of rhythm as if sputtering before stopping for good. In those moments, Dionisio would feel his head twirling, he could not breath and everything would turned cloudy. Those were not heart attacks; the doctors at least knew that. During those episodes, as his mom would call them, Dionisio would see among the cloudiness a vision: a light skinned woman's face, beautiful, with black eyes. She would smile and nod. Dionisio knew that that woman was The Death, waiting for him, patiently. Sometimes he would see himself in the visions, in a strange body, not his, that made him feel very different. Visions would not last for too long, but long enough to leave Dionisio in a state of confusion. The Death allowed Dionisio to have sporadic and brief episodes, at least three per year. At the beginning, when he was young, his parents watched him suffer and had no idea how to help him. After several episodes, Mr. and Mrs. Diosdado realized the episodes were not critical, and so they stopped obsessing about them. The doctors prescribed Dionisio a large number of different pills, capsules, and even suppositories hopping to alleviate his symptoms. The poor kid was like a walking pharmacy. He would take them daily, religiously. When the episode would come, the doctor would change the medicines that lasted until the next episode. Many types of medication would march through Dionisio's medicine drawer until the day that his parents decided that all the medicine that Dionisio had taken had the same effect as water with sugar, and therefore, he stopped taking them at the beginning of his teenage years.

"Poor baby! Does your heart hurt when you have an episode?" asked Claudia with consternation.

"No, it doesn't hurt, I just feel my heart beating at a different rhythm. It's weird, I can't describe the feeling. But don't worry, I'm used to having them. I don't worry much about them anymore."

"May I listen to it?"

"My heart?" asked Dionisio, somewhat confused, "I guess it's ok but I doubt you will hear anything but my normal heartbeat."

Claudia got closer and very carefully placed her right arm over Dionisio's back while placing her right ear on his chest. Dionisio started to get nervous and looked both ways to see if someone was watching them, but the bridge was empty. Claudia's hair touched his chin and her perfume ascended until it reached his nose; it was a fresh scent, discreet and a bit sweet and citrusy like a magnolia flower's scent. He felt her hand pressing against his back. Dionisio's heart became agitated, not like in an episode, but because he was excited about having that woman listening to his chest. He lifted his eyes and saw the ocean at the distance, a sunny day and calm; almost hidden because of the day light was a faint moon. The moon's image entered his black eyes to flood his vision, his mind, and then it went directly to his heart. It responded by beating new beats that he had never felt before, as if the heart were pumping in opposite direction. Claudia listened to the beats and soon realized that those sounds were not related to Dionisio's sickness or episodes, they were not even related to Dionisio himself; those heartbeats were hers, Claudia's, resonating in Dionisio's rib cage, inside that man that she barely knew. Dionisio did not stop looking at the moon until he felt that those heartbeats were not his; were they Claudia's? He felt dizzy and separated himself from her. She almost fell over.

"I am sorry," said Dionisio, "I am not feeling well…physically…I need to leave…"

"I understand," interrupted Claudia, who was also recovering from what had just happened, "see you tomorrow."

They did not see each other the next day because neither of them showed up at the bridge, and that lasted for a few days. Despite the mutual separation, both thought about each other, almost uncontrollably.

Dionisio dreamed with a heavy snow fall punishing a great valley surrounded by sharp mountains stretching towards the cloud cover. In the middle, large buffaloes trotted rhythmically chasing a visible orange scent, and in the sky, in a brief opening among the snow-spitting clouds, the moon sieved itself; the same moon that he saw the day when he heard that woman's heartbeat inside of him.

That same night, Claudia made love under her fiancé's pelvis. But she did not feel her heat wave that always flooded her body; she could not see the orange orchard, she was not flying above the trees, the fruit scent non-existent. Claudia reached an empty and ephemeral climax. She was not satisfied. She felt vain and lacking. In her mind, she heard her own heart beating inside that man's body. She saw him when she was falling asleep, at the same time that an orange scent entered her sleep.

Part 6

His name was Rómulo, a heavy guy with a very curvy belly and very dark brown skin that made him look more like a wart-less toad. He also had greasy curly hair. He lost the genetic lottery. On top of that, he wore glasses with a thick black frame. However, he had a superb memory (he had to have something positive) and loved to preach his encyclopedic knowledge to anyone that would stand him. Among these very few people was Claudia. She was fascinated with intelligent men that could talk for hours and with extreme detail and confidence about any specific topic. Rómulo Ramírez could talk like that, but he was arrogant and his physical appearance did not help him much; most people preferred to avoid him. Claudia, on the contrary, was as attracted to him as flies to honey

"What do see in that guy? He is horrible and looks like a toad." Ivette, her best friend from high school would tell her.

"You are so superficial! Look at him, he is very smart, he can talk for hours and hours about any topic, eloquently, with exquisite logic. And, the physical appearance is the least concern about a person; one should look on the inside, which is what matters."

"Oh my, Claudia, it's your life. But this guy is really ugly."

She met him in class, a philosophy class. Rómulo would argue intensely over every topic that the professor would put in front of the class. He quickly became the teacher's pet and sometimes it appeared that the class was only taught to him. From the first moment, Claudia was hypnotized by that eloquent man. She approached him bravely, introduced herself, and chatted for a few hours about anything. Claudia, who was as intelligent as Rómulo, but not as good at expressing it as him, was completely mesmerized by him. That first interaction ended by Claudia saying goodbye with a kiss on his cheek, which on purpose was on the corner of the lips. She enjoyed that kiss. Rómulo did not. From that very moment, he knew that Claudia would admire and adore him. He liked to talk with her, he accepted her invitations to have coffee or something after classes. She was absorbed with him. Rómulo felt like a god, a very ugly god.

"You are in love." her grandmother informed her.

"Oh, Nana, why do you say that?"

"Why? Because I know things. And your eyes tell everything, they look as if you have just descended from heaven."

Claudia reddened.

"Don't worry child. Let's just keep this between us, do not mention it to your grandpa…he may not understand it well. But tell me, who is this man?"

Claudia described this ordinary man to her grandmother, and she became proud of how her granddaughter had such great taste.

"How did you fall in love with Rómolo the toad? One thing is that he was intelligent, but another thing is to have bad taste."

"You know what? Sometimes you are a pill."

"A pill? You always give me a hard time about what I want, and I always give you a hard time about what you want or about your tantrums."

"That's what you think," said Claudia, "but one day I will stop talking to you and I am going to forget all about you."

"Sure, I really want to see that." Dionisio answered mockingly.

Claudia looked at him. She knew he was right. She allowed Dionisio, and only Dionisio, any type of behavior. Not even her fiancé had this kind of liberty with her.

"I'm leaving!" exclaimed a very upset Claudia.

When she turned to leave to her building, Dionisio, to prove that he was right, slapped her beautiful butt cheek. Her wrath turned her face red, and without saying a word, she cursed him. But she did not turn to face him. She knew that he was allowed to have that type of physical contact with her. Claudia had begged him many times to stop touching her in inappropriate ways, but at the same time, deep inside of her, she hoped that he would not stop. To her, it was comforting to know that someone had such an obsession with her body.

Dionisio bragged to himself about the freedom he had with her, that he could touch Claudia whenever he wanted. He did it because he liked it, even when she pleaded for him not to; he believed he had an innate right to do it.

For almost a year, Rómulo let Claudia chase him. During a school party, at a friend's house, both of them found themselves in the privacy of an empty room. Rómulo took Claudia in his arms and tried to kiss her. Claudia did not resist, she thought that finally the day when Rómulo would declare his love for her had arrived. When their lips touched Claudia took a good and detailed look at him: she realized he was, indeed, ridiculously ugly at sight. At that very moment, Claudia forgot the logic of his Solomonic arguments, his intelligence, his photographic memory, and saw him like the toad he was, a toad that will not turn into a prince after the kiss. Rómulo brought her closer to him for Claudia to feel his body. She became nauseated. She tried to break free but he resisted. He kept kissing her and in Claudia's mind she saw herself mounted by that amphibious man than besieged her. She did not know how to act, she did not want to lose her virginity to that monster of the Black Lagoon, she did not want to get pregnant and deliver tadpoles or axolotls. Suddenly, the opportunity came when he released his grip, at that moment Claudia kicked him hard in the testicles. Rómulo freed her and fell to the floor rolling in pain. Claudia fled the room. Music and cigarette smoke filled the house. Some people were dancing, others chatted, but no one saw Claudia. She ran right through the middle of all the guests. She went to a corner, looked for her purse and sweater, and when she found them she left the house as fast as she possibly could. Rómulo recovered himself, came out of the room angry as a bullfrog. He did not see her anymore that night. After the incident, he tried to look for her at school, but Claudia had the goal of avoiding him. Many months passed for Rómulo to forget the incident. Claudia never did.

"That is why you like me, because I am ugly and remind you of the toad."
"You aren't ugly, I have said that many times. You are a handsome man and surely many women are attracted to you."
"But you are not attracted to me."
Claudia pretended to ignore the comment, but could not.
"Your silence affirms what I certainly know." said Dionisio ambiguously.

Years later, Rómulo was found dead on a cheap motel bed. His naked body extended like a frog or a toad ready to be dissected. He was the victim of a prostitute that robbed him, or at least that was the official line. Claudia never found out about his death.

Part 7

"Do you know what is the best part of this school?" Alfonso asked.

"No, I don't." answered Dionisio.

"That at least after three years here you would have fucked a girl."

Dionisio did not know how to answer that promising forecast. Ena had left him with a deep wound in his sentimental heart and very low self-esteem. He spent most of the summer trying to forget her but his efforts ended up with her constantly on his mind. The warm and humid nights in La Costa, his mind flooded with Ena and the shame she cast on him in front of all those classmates; it was a good recipe for a constant insomnia. He became isolated with no friends, and turned to imaginary girls that caused him young and hard erections that he never knew how to satisfy. He was not handsome, but he knew he was not too bad either. He was still developing but at least he grew a few inches during that summer. Despite his solitude, physically, he felt great; far was the day that his heart gave him trouble the last time and he did not recall the day when he was sick of anything else. Mr. and Mrs. Diosdado saw their kid in such good shape that they took him to the mountains to breathe a clearer and fresher air. Dionisio enjoyed those vacations a lot and they made him forget about what had happened with Ena. It was there, on the side of the mountains, that he saw snow for the first time in his life: white, pure, untampered. He wondered how it was possible that something like water could turn into a crystalline, cold and beautiful particle that upon contact with warm skin would renounce to its solid state and become a water droplet. To him, snow was magical.

Alfonso Murieta, a direct descendent of Spaniards, was a young kid that lived closed to the Diosdado's house. Dionisio did not know him well, he barely talked to him except for the times that Dionisio would go to the small convenience store Alfonso's parents owned close by. One day, in the middle of September, Dionisio went to buy some pastries and met Alfonso, who was tending the store. In that occasion, Alfonso found out that Dionisio would attend the same school as Alfonso, and he decided to share his knowledge of it with Dionisio. A very superficial friendship was born out of that small chat. Alfonso had his driver's license by that time, and every now and then would take Dionisio to school. Alfonso loved listening to himself talk and he would monopolize every conversation with Dionisio. Most of what he talked about was about sexual issues: how to flirt with girls, what was the simplest way to take them to the back seat of the car, or if lucky, to take them to a bed, which according to Alfonso, by nature is the most comfortable situation but lacks the adventure spirit of making out inside the car with the chance of being observed by any passerby. Dionisio was young and his nascent sexual hormone waves made Alfonso seem like an idol. It was interesting to him that Alfonso, who was not handsome at all, but fat, pale white, and lacked grace, knew so much about women. His hopes of bedding a girl were very high.

It took a few weeks for Dionisio to find out that Alfonso was a charlatan. He talked so much about women but had zero actual experience with them.

Paola was a short girl with a very annoying voice, but she was extremely beautiful. She was in the second year of high school. Dionisio met her through a mutual acquaintance and liked her personality very much: she spoke sweetly, which help forgetting about her horrible squeaky voice. Suddenly, Dionisio's solitude and imaginary friends vacated his soul and he instead started thinking about Paola. He enjoyed her company and spending time with her. One October day, in the middle of the morning, Alfonso met Dionisio and Paola who were chatting. When Paola left them to go to a class, Alfonso mentioned to Dionisio that Paola was a great whore and that he had fucked her at least three times. Dionisio's eyes turned red of anger, and yelled at Alfonso that he was a stupid Spaniard charlatan, because Paola just moved to La Costa this year, and had not met Alfonso until this October day. Alfonso did not know how to respond. It was true, Alfonso had not had sex with Paola or any other girl for that matter. Not even one single girl had said yes to his innuendos. His only satisfaction was to pleasure himself with cheap pornographic magazines. Dionisio never talked to him again; Dionisio avoided him, he even tried to go to a farther convenience store to avoid meeting Alfonso. However, that initial conversation he had with him never departed his mind during those three years he spent in high school. His hormones decided to be with as many girls as possible. Long gone were the days when he felt miserable because of Ena.

The chats he had with Paola made Dionisio realize that he had a powerful tool at his disposal: his talking. Dionisio started flirting and telling Paola about her assets. He was not lying, he simply talked to her nicely and beautifully. He would say, for example, that she possessed in her short being all what a man needed. That way, slowly but surely, Dionisio won Paola's heart. They started a relationship that turned out to be brief but full of youthful passion. They would hug and kiss anywhere without paying attention to the judging people around them. They talked constantly and Dionisio would promise her the moon and the stars. Paola loved his lips and eyes, may be the only positive physical attributes that little piece of man had, but above all, she fell in love with the wonderful and enchanting way he talked to her.

"I think I love you." Paola said to Dionisio.

He did not know what to say, she took him by surprise. He looked directly at her eyes for a few seconds and with a calculated coldness he replied, "I do not." Dionisio turned around and left. Paola stood there until tears flooded her face. Dionisio arrived home as if nothing had happened, laid on his bed and started laughing enthusiastically.

"Hello."
"Hello."
"I have not seen you for a few days."
"Yes, I have been busy."
"Me too."

Silence came. Both of them were looking at the ocean and the gray rainy day above it. Waves were agitated.

"Well, I have to go." said Claudia.

"No, wait…don't go, why the rush?" Dionisio said turning towards her.

"No rush."

Dionisio did not answer. They looked at each other and then turned back their eyes to the ocean. Finally, with butterflies in his gut, Dionisio spoke.

"What did you feel?"

"What are you talking about?" Claudia feigned ignorance.

"When you listened to my heart."

Claudia did not want to answer; the conversation was somewhat uncomfortable to her. She thought about Juan Carlos and all the love she felt for him.

"Have I mentioned I am engaged?" asked Claudia sharply.

"No, I know little about you. Why do you ask me that?"

"I have to go now." Claudia said.

"No, you can't," complained Dionisio.

She looked at him annoyed and a bit upset. Her face turned red.

"Who do you think you are to tell me what I can or cannot do?"

"Who do you think you are to come here and interrupt my lunch almost every day? Was it not obvious that I wanted to be alone, watching the sea, just by myself? But no, you come here interrupting me with that beautiful smile on your face, with those dreamy eyes and that gorgeous silhouette. And now that I decided to ask you something you leave?" replied Dionisio, not very courteous.

Too late, Dionisio realized what he had just said. Claudia was still there, looking at him with an ambiguous expression; was she upset or embarrassed? A short but eternal silence fell on them.

"I am very sorry," Claudia humbly said, "you are right, I never thought you wanted to be alone. I invaded your privacy."

She turned around.

"Wait!"

Dionisio took her by the shoulder and by instinct Claudia moved her hand closer to his. They touched for a few seconds. Claudia suddenly awoke from that episode, then turned around and left with a rush while Dionisio followed her with his sight.

The following day the sky was clear and the sun warmed the city. People gathered in the plaza below the two towers to welcome the sun that had been absent for several days. They drank juices or coffee, some standing, other sitting on public metallic chairs. Claudia was sitting on one of them, concentrated on some paper she was reading. The sun caressed her body and she enjoyed it until a shadow eclipsed the sun. It was him. It took her a moment to recognize who he was; it was strange to see him outside the context of the bridge. He came closer and asked her if he could sit down on the chair beside hers. Claudia nodded.

"What are you doing?"

"Revising some work stuff," she answered, looking at the documents in her hand.

"I want to tell you something."

"Sure."

"I want to be your friend."

Claudia looked at him as if he were a young child.

"That is fine with me," replied Claudia, without enthusiasm.

"And I want to ask you one thing as well."

"Sure, tell me."

"I know what happened the day you listened to my heart, and I also know what happened yesterday. We need to be careful. I believe we may become attracted to each other, want each other, even fall in love. And what I ask you is that, if any of these happens, that you let me know. And I promise to let you know if the same happens to me.

What the fuck is this asshole telling me? thought Claudia, indignantly. She ignored him.

"It's true, I believe you and I have the possibility to attract each other and when that happens, we need to talk about it to avoid it." Dionisio continued casually.

"Avoid what?" interrupted Claudia, annoyed, thinking that she preferred to concentrate herself in the documents than in this man's nonsense talk.

"To avoid a mutual attraction." Dionisio answered.

She did not reply, but it was true, from the moment she met Dionisio, she noticed closeness and an aura of familiarity around him. But attraction? Now that she was engaged to the man that she was fully in love with?

"Ok, I don't want to take more of your time. Thanks for listening to me."

Dionisio stood and left. Claudia looked at him and the only thing that came to mind was "asshole."

Part 8

"Juan Carlos, that is my fiancé's name. He's a lawyer. I love him dearly and from the moment he entered my life I have felt complete. He is also an incredible person, with a life history that has made him what he is today. Why the fuck did you come to ask me to warn you that I may be falling in love with you?"

Claudia was not recognizable, that simple and nice lady that interrupted Dionisio many times was now in front of him defiant, almost ready to slap him on the face. Her eyes were dripping tears of anger and her face reddened. Her veins pulsed, she felt her blood rushing.

"Good morning," answered Dionisio, trying to control the situation and gain some time to process what was going on.

"Don't good morning me! Who do you think you are? If I came to interrupt your lunch it was because I saw you lonely in the bridge and not because I considered you someone to fall in love with. Believe this, I truly love my Juan Carlos and I would never leave him for any other man and especially not an arrogant man such as yourself!" Dionisio looked at her somewhat scared while thinking what to respond, but at that moment any logical answer was very far away from him. He did not take his eyes away from her and noticed something peculiar, not in her physical appearance or her eyes full of tears, it was something else that reflected in the salted sea of her eyes: it was his own image reflecting on hers. And his reflection transformed into hers, making it hard to know what he was seeing.

"Why are you looking at me like that?" said a very upset Claudia.

He did not answer and kept his eyes on her until deep inside of him he felt the need to touch that woman once more. With that in his mind, he moved to cover the three steps separating him from her, and with one swift move he enclosed her with his arms in a rather awkward hug. Claudia was speechless; her initial reaction was to get away from that man, she shook a little trying to get loose. When Dionisio felt her rejection, he let her go. But she did not. Far away over the ocean, the seagulls flew in large circles under the warming sun. One, two, three circles, and then dove into the ocean for food. One seagull reached its prey with its sharp beak; the fish was trapped, squiggling trying to escape with no use; the fish wanted freedom, wanted to live a little more, but its end was there: its wet scales shone when the sun's rays touched them, a beautiful animal before its death. The Death granted that fish beauty before departing to the other side. The fish shook when the air asphyxiated it; the dryness of this new environment was foreign to the fish. The seagull climbed up in the air enjoying and finishing its meal. A few minutes later, the seagull had forgotten about the fish she ate.

Slowly, both of them stepped back, Dionisio rubbing her arms with his hand in direction to her waist, then her back and finally just in the boundary between her hips and the firm and promising butt cheek. Claudia felt every single move but neither moved nor said a word. Her face no longer showed signs of anger and her eyes were free of tears. Silence spoke for them and in its immensity, both heard each other for the first time.

Part 9

"Sometimes I wonder whether we have met before, like being together in the same place without noticing each other."

"What do you mean?"

"I mean, maybe when we were kids we were in the same place, a park, a movie theater; we were close to each other without knowing that in the future we would finally meet each other and have this relationship."

"This relationship?"

"Well, friendship or whatever," Dionisio answered, "but don't change the topic, do you understand what I'm saying?"

Claudia pretended to think hard about it.

"I think I know what you mean. But you were raised here in La Costa and I grew up in Salamanca, the chances of having been in the same place at the same time when kids are very low…however," Claudia stopped because a memory crossed her mind.

"However, what?"

"…I was in La Costa when I was a kid, before my parents' death," said Claudia, as if something was becoming visible in her mind, "we came here on vacation, I was a kid, maybe 5 years old."

"Then we were in the same city without noticing it."

"True, but what is special about that?"

"Nothing, I just sometimes think about that."

"Well, that is really stupid. But now that I remember, when we came here there was a kite flying race at the beach. Yes, I can see it clearly now…there were so many different kites, I have never seen that many together in the same place. And there was one that was really special, Japanese or Chinese, with a wide and very long tail, like five or 10 meters long, yellow, and the main body of the kite was black." Dionisio looked at her suspiciously.

"What?"

The next day Dionisio called Claudia from his office.

"I have something to show you, can you come to the bridge now?"

"Now? I am kind of busy."

"Yes, now."

Claudia was a bit annoyed because of the interruption, but agreed.

Five minutes later, Claudia's silhouette entered the bridge. At the end was Dionisio with a yellow envelop in his hand.

"Ok, here I am, show me."

Dionisio stretched his arm and gave the envelop to her. Not very convinced, Claudia opened it and from inside she retrieved a normal size photograph. When Claudia looked at the photograph her eyes widened.

"I can't believe it." was the only thing she said.

The day was just sunny, not a single cloud was in sight in the blue dome covering that April weekend. It was hot but bearable, especially with the sea breeze. The beach was full of a multitude that came because of the Holy Week. The sea was a soup of people of different colors and shapes, some jumping the blue waves, others floating or swimming. In the middle of the beach there was a banner indicating that the First Kite Flying Race was being held that day. Most of the participants were parents with their kids, all happy to be there. Mr. Diosdado always showed an interest for anything that could fly: airplanes, helicopters, rockets, but kites were something even more special to him. He could not miss the race and decided to take Dionisio: he thought that the poor sickly kid would benefit from the experience. Dionisio's dad wanted to participate in the race and decided to get a kite, but not any regular type of kite: he wanted the winning kite, the one that could fly the highest and the most beautiful to the sight. Thus, weeks before the event he contacted many stores in different Chinatowns across and outside the country until he found what he was looking for: a spectacular kite with a wide, yellow and very long tail, and a black pentagon body. At the beach, Mr. Diosdado, proudly and delicately took the kite out of the box. First the long tail that little Dionisio helped his dad by pulling it out, and then the head. People started gathering around to see that monster kite, something that Mr. Diosdado expected and was joyfully enjoying. Some asked Mr. Diosdado where the kite came from, or whether he had flown it before, or whether it was capable of flying at all. Mr. Diosdado answered all those questions as a real aficionado, without noticing that Dionisio was playing with the tail, and while doing that he was wrapping himself in it. At the same time, a little girl, around the same age, came close to him smiling. Both of them looked at each other and then a click from Mrs. Diosdado's camera; she had come unexpectedly to the beach.

The day ended disappointedly for Mr. Diosdado: the kite never flew. It turned out that the tail was too heavy and regardless of how fast he ran, he never made the kite to be more than two meters above the sand.

It is very simple: only three persons are in the foreground, while out of focus there is a great number of people around them. A man and two kids. The sea is blue and the day is bright. Far away one can see people playing on the waves. The man is showing part of a yellow and black kite to someone outside of the frame. A boy is holding the kite's tail, which is wrapped around his tiny tadpole-like body. The girl is looking at the boy, directly at his eyes. The boy looks at her as if looking into a mirror. This is when the photograph does its magic: the two kids are almost identical, although it is obvious that one is a boy and the other a girl, the latter being in much better health. The same, but different.

“Did you know I was the one on the photo?” asked Claudia concerned.

“What do you mean?” answered Dionisio surprised.

“I don’t know, but that is me! You see what I see right?”

“What do you see?”

“Don’t mess with me, you clearly know what I am talking about.”

“I’ll tell you, I have never paid much attention to this photo. I got it from one of my parent’s albums from their house. I recalled the photo when you mentioned you were at the Flying Kite Race and saw a long and yellow kite. I thought it was an interesting coincidence. I went to my parent’s house, retrieved the photo and looked at it in detail, I got goosebumps. And there you were! How would I have known it was you before even meeting you?”

“It just doesn’t make sense that you and I looked alike, like twins.”

“No, it does not make sense. My parents never told me anything about the girl in the photo that looks like me. Maybe they never realized it?”

“How come no one realized that the two kids look identical, it is very obvious!”

There was a pause while Claudia thought for a second.

“I know, let me have the photo and I’ll show it to Juan Carlos and see what he thinks.”

“Show it to your better half?”

“Don’t start, I don’t want to play your games.”

“Let me show you something that I found. Look.”

“Where did you get this photo?”

"That doesn't matter. Look at it well, and tell me is you find something interesting or striking."

Juan Carlos looked at it for a few seconds, moving the photo from one side to the other to have a better look.

"I think it is a kite, and if it is, then it is pretty large, especially the tail."

"Yes, but that isn't it, take a very good look at it, a good one!" said Claudia, jumping like a little excited girl.

"The kite's tail is wrapped around the boy?" answered Juan Carlos with very little confidence.

"No, seriously Juan Carlos, pay attention!"

Juan Carlos kept analyzing the picture, but not with less enthusiasm than before. He knew that he was not going to find what Claudia wanted, but even so, he made a good effort, or at least pretended to do it.

"I know! It is the beach where we swam for the first time when we moved to La Costa."

Claudia stared at him merciless.

"For crying out loud, look at the kids!! Can you see them? Do you see it?"

"Claudia, please, I have no idea what you want me to see! One is a boy and the other a girl?" said a frustrated Juan Carlos.

"The kids are identical, they look like twins! And I am the girl!" screamed Claudia.

Juan Carlos revised the photo one more time, moving it sideways to get a better angle.

"No, that isn't you. I have seen pictures of you when you were a kid and the one in this photo is not you. Also, the two kids are completely different, why do you say they look the same?"

"Look at it!! It's obvious those two kids look like twins, or at least they resemble each other."

"I think we need to adjust your medicines, you are hallucinating." joked Juan Carlos.

Claudia took the photo away from him and dashed out of the room, slamming the door.

Part 10

Claudia studied chemical engineering, not because she had a passion for the subject, but mostly because she wanted to be away from her family; she felt her grandparents were asphyxiating her. She dreamed of being free. Chemical engineering was not a major that could be studied in any university in Salamanca, but in Monserrat, a few hundred kilometers away from the capital city. To her, that distance from her family was ideal. She climbed on the bus that would take her to Monserrat, from the window she waved her hand at her grandparents, aunts, uncles, and cousins that where there to wish her well; that was the last time she saw her grandparents alive. The grandmother died of a fulminant stroke that only granted her a few hours of life in the intensive care unit. Claudia came immediately to Salamanca when she heard the news. A few months later, Claudia was again in the capital when her grandfather passed away, most likely of loneliness and lost love. At the cemetery, under an overcast, windy, and cold day, Claudia cried for almost an hour for her parents and grandparents. She could not believe that four of the people that she loved most in her life had vanished early in her youth. When she finished crying, she took a white rose from one of the wreaths, plucked the petals off, and threw them on top of the tombs. Her heart was empty.

Monserrat turned into a grey and dark city for Claudia. She dedicated most of her time to her studies to forget her pain. She succeeded in college, but her relationship with the rest of her family was abysmal; she would not call them by phone nor answer their calls. On a few occasions, one or two of her cousins would go to Monserrat to visit her and check that she was doing well. She would welcome them with enthusiasm and would put herself in the best possible mood. In reality, she enjoyed those visits. As time passed, the gray Monserrat started gaining some color, especially when Claudia decided to come to closure with her parents' and her grandparents' deaths. Still, she would dream about them, she missed them dearly and thought about them fondly; but their absence was not a heavy load anymore.

Claudia rediscovered her freedom and bathed in it. The first thing she discovered was alcohol, and how relaxing she felt under its influence. She drank every weekend and with little moderation. Initially, she would vomit breakfast, lunch, and dinner, and would wake up disoriented in the small room she rented or at a friend's house. Eventually, her body got used to her drinking, she was able to do it without feeling lost or blacking out. Of course, during this period, her studies suffered considerably and she obtained some of the worst grades in her academic life. Claudia knew that she was in the wrong, that alcohol was not her friend and that it would only lead her to something tragic; but at the same time, she would say to herself that she could stop anytime she wanted. That did not happen as such. The reason that led her to stop was a liver intoxication that took her to the hospital for a few days. Doctors reprimanded her and told her that either she stops drinking, or at least drink with a lot of moderation, or she would end up in an early grave. Claudia was scared to the bones, so much that she never drank a single glass of any alcoholic beverage until years later when she drank with Dionisio at the beach.

Claudia was not interested in dating, but that did not stop her heat waves. On the contrary, she felt them more powerful, making her think that it would only be a matter of time until she would auto-combust. She found, or rediscovered, her body as more mature in the solitude of her room, and realized that she was a great lover to herself. She would travel frequently to the orange orchards, and the orangey smell of her orgasms was so intense that every time she would get into her room, the aroma would hit her on the nose. That stimulated her to enter into a cycle of pleasure.

In the fourth year of the five that she lived in Monserrat, Claudia met Juan Carlos Tilapia at a party. Juan Carlos studied law and was a close friend to Sabrina, a thin, dark browned skinny girl with a very delicate body that radiated men-stopping-sensuality, and who was also a good friend of Claudia's. Sabrina asked Claudia more than once why she did not have a boyfriend, being such an incredible woman and knowing that there was more than one guy after her. Claudia would answer that she did not need them, and that was true.

"Is there something about Sabrina that you don't want to tell me?" asked Dionisio with curiosity.

"I have told you the most relevant about her, there is nothing else to say."

"I may look like a fool but I ain't one. You have told me with extensive detail the life of all your friends but Sabrina, she has always been left apart. I know she was one of your best friends in college and that is why I wonder why you do not tell me more details about her."

"There is nothing else to tell," said Claudia, trying to redirect the conversation.

"Let me think for a minute…I know! I bet you slept with her!" Dionisio said, throwing the accusation as a probe.

Claudia was taken by surprise by that comment. She did not know how to answer and instead her cheeks turned red as a tomato.

"I knew it!" said a victorious Dionisio, "c'mon, tell me the details."

"Please notice that I am ignoring you." said Claudia turning her back at him.

Dionisio stared at her figure, the day light filtering through the bridge windows hitting her butt and legs. He envied to be those rays.

"Don't be like that; I have told you a lot of things about me. It is your turn."

"It isn't my turn!"

"C'mon!"

"No!"

"Please?"

"No, and stop asking me or I will leave."

Dionisio got close to her, held her shoulders and brought his nose close to her neck. He smelled it. Claudia was surprised, but at the same moment she wanted him and a new heat wave started to grow. Claudia turned around to free herself. When she did, she saw him so close to her that it would take half a second to touch his lips with hers. She resisted, but her mind was somewhere else.

"Tell me," Dionisio insisted.

Claudia gave in, as she would frequently do when she faced that man's charges. She would fight within herself, but it was useless. Something about Dionisio was too powerful.

Claudia told him that she met Sabrina during the days the alcohol had control of her. They were at a party, they drank together and told each other their lives. The party turned south, a fight started that rapidly escalated with a guy pulling out a gun. Claudia and Sabrina left the party as fast as they could, along with most of other guests. In the street, Sabrina told Claudia that the party should continue in her apartment. Claudia nodded and both left. There was no attraction among the two of them and there never was, especially because the two of them were heterosexuals to the bone. That night, they drank and chatted in Sabrina's bed. They ended up falling sleep hugging each other. In the middle of the night Claudia flew on top of the orange orchards but that time she found Sabrina's body. They did not know who kissed who first or who started touching the other in remote places, but what they did know was that, in said night, both of them lost their virginity, if that can be called as such. Once sober, they swore each other not to talk a word about it and to leave it in the past for their friendship's sake. However, both of them would recall that episode in their minds, and would always smile about it.

Years later, Sabrina was found dead inside a bathtub in the company of another woman. Both had signs of struggle but the cause of death was unknown.

"I knew it, you are a very horny woman!"

"And you are an asshole, that's the last time I tell you my private moments because you just make fun of me."

"I am not making fun."

"Yes, you are, and I bet you also had experiences with men."

"Those files, if they exist, are closed forever. But you and Sabrina! Incredible!"

"Don't even think about it. I do not do that. I know what you are thinking."

"No, I would not do that with you. I would not share you with another woman. I want to enjoy you by myself."

Claudia pretended as if the comment were never said, but inside of her, the heat wave was as hungry as a wolf and was looking for anything to satisfy it. Claudia needed to get out of his presence fast. She said goodbye with the excuse of some unfinished business at work. Once in her office and with the door closed, Claudia flew one more time above the orange trees.

Part 11

Juan Carlos entered Claudia's life precipitously. Neither of them wanted a romantic relationship with the other. After the party where they had met, there were several phone calls that both initiated. They would have long conversations where Juan Carlos would tell Claudia stupid stories that made her laugh to the point of almost peeing herself. The phone call conversations proceeded without any of the two suggesting to go out for a coffee, to the movies or just to stroll in the park. Juan Carlos confessed to Claudia that he was seeing a girl named Esther, who he was fond of and thought that everything he was looking for was encapsulated in her. Claudia took it well, and told him that at the moment she was not looking to have a romantic relationship, which may have had some truth and some lie to it.

Juan Carlos was a Monserrat native, the only child of very poor parents who fought all their lives for Juan Carlos to have whatever needed to be someone in life. Both parents worked several jobs, and when Juan Carlos was a teenager, he decided to work in anything possible to help his parents. At the beginning, both parents rejected the idea of him working, but after a few weeks of intense lobbying, his parents gave in to the idea of Juan Carlos finding a job with the explicit condition that any significant drop in his school grades would be enough to stop his idea of working. Very quickly, he found a job at a local newspaper press, not far away from his home. He would come home from school, eat a quick meal, do homework, and then rush proudly to his new job. His job was simple: stack and wrap newspapers with a string for the evening edition. Not an easy job as the description may suggest, especially because the newspaper stacks were heavy and needed to be ready by five in the afternoon. His hands ended up stained with smelly black ink. At the end of the shift, Juan Carlos would go back home, eat a small snack, and then go directly to bed.

His school grades never suffered and his boss was very happy with his performance. When he got paid, he would save one half and the other half would go directly to his parents to help with whatever was needed at home. The first time he did, Mrs. Tilapia ended up in tears while his father hugged him for a long time.

Juan Carlos worked in the newspaper press for almost a year. Then he worked as an assistant to a carpenter with one of his father's friends. He learned many skills and he received a higher salary than what he got at the press. However, after six months, the carpenter business was not as profitable and his boss let him go. Sometime after, one of his best friends from his high school asked him to walk to his dad's law firm. His friend's dad, a thin and expressionless man that loved wearing three-piece black suits, which made him look more like a funeral director than a lawyer, received both teenagers' visit very enthusiastically, and proceed to explain, mostly to Juan Carlos, what a lawyer does, especially in the field of wills, inheritance, and any other aspect related to dead people. The friend's father was impressed with the questions Juan Carlos' asked, which led the father to ask him if he wanted to work filing documents and learn more about what the firm did. Juan Carlos, without thinking twice and with a big smile on his face, accepted the offer. Navarrete was the name of the firm.

Juan Carlos excelled at his job at the firm. He lasted just a few months filing documents before Mr. Navarrete asked him to revise legal documents, comment on them, and ask what he would do in specific cases. When Juan Carlos finished high school, the decision to study law was very simple. The law major fit him very well; he enjoyed every class, and his passion, logic, reasoning, and debating skills put him above most of his classmates. He kept his job at Mr. Navarrete's firm and to save money, he decided to keep living with his parents during the first year of college, but during the second year he moved to an apartment outside the university. It was during the second year that Mr. Navarrete passed away, and his son José Navarrete, Juan Carlos's high school friend, who by that time worked as a funeral director, prepared a beautiful ceremony for his late dad. At the wake, Juan Carlos met one of Mr. Navarrete's old friends, Mr. Archundia. He also had a law firm, but he was a criminal lawyer. Mr. Archundia invited Juan Carlos to visit his firm and after that visit he offered him a position. He accepted and worked with Mr. Archundia for a few years when through a collaboration between two firms, he met the Negro Legorrea. The Negro Legorrea, which after meeting Juan Carlos realized the potential of this young lawyer, proposed to him an incredible offer at his nationwide firm that Mr. Archundia begged Juan Carlos not to squander. Claudia, who at this point was already dating Juan Carlos, was very proud of him.

Despite Juan Carlos' academic and professional success, his intimate love life was not very satisfying. He met Román Romero in high school, a short, stocky boy with a professional fool face that talked as if he had an unknown mental issue that drove everyone insane. Both kids, Juan Carlos and Román Romero, were the worst at sports and met each other when pickup games were organized and both of them were not picked up as part of the teams. They became inseparable friends during high school, and thanks to this relationship, Juan Carlos met Roberta Romero, Román's sister. Roberta, in contrast to her brother, was tall, well built for a woman, with a phenomenal figure and with a face that distilled confidence and fear to anyone that looked directly at her. Anyone that knew Román and Roberta concluded that one of the two was adopted, because it was difficult to believe that there was so much genetic variability among the parents for their kids to be physically in opposite ends of the spectrum. In reality, they were indeed siblings from the same mother and father.

Juan Carlos, as well as nighty percent of the other kids in high school, fell in love with Roberta Romero, but he had the advantage that Román Romero was his closest friend. When Juan Carlos had a free time from school and work, he tried to visit Román with the excuse that he wanted to study with him. Román might have had a fool's face, but he was not one: he knew perfectly well that Juan Carlos came to his house to spy on Roberta. Roberta, on the other hand, knew the power she had over boys and a few grown up men, and she used it as a weapon. On more than one occasion, she sent Juan Carlos to take a cold shower. When Juan Carlos was around the house, Roberta would come out of the shower wrapped in a towel with a well-placed slit that allowed a peek at the promised land. Other times, Roberta would jump on an exercise trampoline right at Juan Carlos' view for him to see all her paired anatomical features move up and down, which hypnotized him as if they were the chants of a sexually deprived siren. Román Romero told Juan Carlos many times that his sister was just playing with him, but Juan Carlos' hormones ignored Román's advice.

One Ash Wednesday, when Juan Carlos did not have to work because he was told to go to mass to have the cross rubbed on his forehead, (which he ignored since he was not religious), he went to Román and Roberta's house. He rang the bell a couple of times, and after waiting for a few minutes and no one opened, he was about to leave when Roberta opened the door showing him her monumental legs hanging from a very short mini skirt that left very little to the imagination. On top of the skirt was a small blue blouse stretching to its maximum due to the endowed and well-rounded breasts threatening to burst out. Her brown face, red lips and long dark hair gave Roberta an untamable and promiscuous aura. His mind had not a single word for Juan Carlos to use at that moment, and only an idiotic guttural sound came out of his mouth. Roberta Romero looked at him, maybe with a little compassion or maybe as someone that she could pulverize with passion, and without saying a word, she grabbed him by the arm and pulled him inside the house where she kissed him with a sensual and passionate kiss, from which Juan Carlos could not and wanted not to escape from. The house was only for the two of them. They ended up on a sofa, they touched and kissed more. But something was wrong, Juan Carlos could not feel his sexual organ to be awake. Maybe I need to be further aroused, he lied to himself. More hugs, more touching, more kissing, and Juan Carlos was still far away from ready. Roberta, on the other hand was all prepared to welcome him; she asked him to make her his. He froze in place. She asked again without knowing that Juan Carlos was losing the most painful battle of his life. When Roberta Romero finally realized what was the problem, Juan Carlos was already weeping.

Visits to Román Romero's house became less frequent. Román thought his sister had done something to Juan Carlos, but never asked him about it. Despite this episode, they remained very good friends.

Before meeting Claudia, Juan Carlos had a couple of girlfriends. He tried to make love to both of them, but the fear of a similar episode occurring made him lose concentration and resulted in too early discharges. His girlfriends loved him very much because in reality, he was a great person: handsome, intelligent, and with a lot of potential. But lacking satisfaction in the bedroom left both of his ex-girlfriends wanting, which ended the relationship. Esther, the third girlfriends, thought about it twice, and when she was about to leave him, Claudia got in the way. Claudia ignored it and was not troubled by Juan Carlos' subpar performance in the bedroom; she was happy knowing she could combine sex with him and her trips to the orange orchards. She never minded that he would end first because she could fly away alone, as she had done since she was a kid, to the large expansion of orange trees.

"One day I am going to show you what you have been missing."

"You are horrible!" answered Claudia, "he makes a really good effort. It's a mental issue, you know? And besides, he has many other great assets that make him a superb person."

"Still, one day I will show you what you have been missing and that day your oranges would be so real that you will end up drenched in orange juice." replied Dionisio with a prophetic tone.

Claudia did not answer. She ignored him while she passed her tongue on her lips as if she was anticipating and savoring something delicious but unattainable.

Part 12

They saw each other at another party and despite Esther presence, they were inseparable. Esther looked at them in disbelief and could not understand how her boyfriend was more interested in Claudia than in her. Esther knew about Claudia since Juan Carlos had the habit of telling her everything he did, and never felt threatened or jealous about her. But that night was the exception. Before the party ended, and also because of a fake headache, Juan Carlos took Esther home. On the way, he withstood all sorts of accusations. He said nothing and simply listened to her. Once at her place, he got out of the car, opened the door for her, took her arm and like the true gentleman he was, walked her to the house door, where he kissed her goodnight on the forehead. All this time, Esther kept accusing him until she found herself alone at her house door. Once Esther was safe and sound at home, Juan Carlos went back to the party. He entered the house paying no attention to all the eyes looking at him and wondering where Esther was. He went directly to her, took her by the arm, turned her around, and without hesitation, kissed her in front of everybody at the party that clearly knew about Juan Carlos and Esther's relationship. Claudia did not resist the kiss because it felt like destiny. After that kiss, Juan Carlos took Claudia to his apartment.

Of course, Claudia knew what was making love, or having sex, or fucking, or whatever other name is given to the act where a man and a woman combine themselves in one flesh. From the moment she learned about the act, she had felt a great curiosity about it. First, she was disgusted about the idea that a man, or better said, an appendage of a man would be inside of her, especially because this appendage was the same used for men to pee; *'what happens if he pees inside of me?'* she would think. Therefore, she thought of it as a bad joke that the entire reproduction capacity of the human race depended on that gross act. As she grew up, Claudia realized that sex was not only a reproductive act, but something that could bring a lot of pleasure. *'Pleasure about what?'* she would ask herself. It took her some time to associate her heat waves with sexual pleasure, and it wasn't until her intimate one-night relationship with Sabrina that she discovered that flying over the orange trees and the sexual act could be combined to become one and the same. Still, she was intrigued about how a penis could satisfy her. She had plenty of girl friends in Monserrat with more sexual experience than her that would assure her that when that day arrives, she would not regret it. These chats helped Claudia fantasize about that day: the moment when someone special, a well-rounded man, would come to her life and fulfill all of her fantasies. And he had to be special, not someone like the toad-looking Rómulo. When Juan Carlos kissed her, she realized that the man that would take her flower had arrived. Kissing and caressing Juan Carlos in his bed, she felt the heat wave building up with intensity, she felt her head spinning and could feel every inch of her skin palpitate. With each kiss Juan Carlos took Claudia deep into the orange orchard where the citric smell was very intense. And then, it happened. Juan Carlos got himself into Claudia's small body, tearing up everything: flesh, oranges, trees. Claudia screamed, something that Juan Carlos confused with pleasure, and so he started moving with more confidence and strength. She froze and let him finish whatever he was doing, something that to her lasted several long minutes, but that in reality were just seconds. The fly over the orange trees was immediately aborted.

Sabrina told Claudia that the first time was the hardest, and that most women feel pain instead of pleasure. But that was not sufficient to convince Claudia, that apart from being physically hurt, she could not walk properly because she still felt Juan Carlos inside, tearing her apart. Despite this rough beginning, Juan Carlos and Claudia established a solid relationship that gradually matured, centered on love and respect. The sex improved, not because of Juan Carlos, that was really bad in bed and always finished with an Olympic speed, but because Claudia combined the act with her trips to the orange trees. Her trips were not as intense as when she traveled alone, but she was pleased with the fact that she could do them in the presence of Juan Carlos. However, until that point in her life, she had never mentioned to him or anyone besides her grandmother, about her orgasmic trips flying over the orange tree tops.

"Why did you tell me about your trips but you have not said a word about them to Juan Carlos?"
"I don't know. I just decided to tell you." answered Claudia to Dionisio hiding her eyes from his.
"That is very interesting. Maybe you want me to fly with you to pick up some oranges."
"You are an asshole." Claudia reproached him.
"Deep inside of you, you want it, girl." answered Dionisio, while he rubbed her butt cheek with his hand without her noticing, or at least she pretended not to notice.

Part 13

Dionisio's options were limited. The state university only provided a handful of majors, none of which he felt any passion for. The decision was between accounting, actuary, and the new major of biomedical engineering. With a simple eenie-meenie-miney-mo, Dionisio sealed his fate and chose biomedical engineering. He did not care much about what to study because he knew that his heart was weak and that his future was not very promising, and thus, anything he would dedicate his life to would only be in vain. But at the same time, he did not want to throw everything overboard and wait for his appointment with The Death lying on his bed. The decision was not bad at all; he found the classes were more interesting and entertaining than he had originally thought. Also, going to college gave him the opportunity to move out of the house he had lived in since he was little. His house had innumerable corners where memories abounded: his room that he kept mostly intact for many years, with the exception of posters of cartoons, music idols, actors, and actresses, that changed as he grew up; the living room that had a black and white television that preceded the transistors age, and despite being non-functional for many years served as an *ad hoc* table; the small yard that he could see from his bedroom window where white geckos, which he detested, would sneak into his room. Despite these memories and knowing that he would leave his house and his parents, the idea of living by himself and starting a new stage in his life was fascinating.

Mr. and Mrs. Diosdado found a cozy one-bedroom apartment with a nice living room and a small storage room on the building's roof. The apartment was close to the university, just off La Decima. It was part of a group of twenty buildings, no more than eight stories each, that formed two large circles of ten buildings each, and in between the circles there was a yard with a playground and other amenities. The apartment complex was cute and a couple of years old, with cobblestone streets and even a security post at the only entrance, with guards trained to greet anyone with good mornings, afternoons, and evenings, and also to lift a metallic arm to let only the tenants' cars enter. The apartment had everything needed to start a new life: furniture, dishes, towels, etc. Dionisio's parents told him that the landlady was a very old widow that had no clue about how much to charge for a monthly rent, and therefore, the price was ridiculously low. Because the rent was insignificant, his parents told him that he was going to be in charge of paying it, and that they would provide him with a monthly stipend. This meant that he would have to find a part time job while studying. Dionisio did not like the agreement much, at least at the beginning, but then he realized that any job, like pizza delivering or receptionist was sufficient to pay the rent and still have enough extra money for his expenses. What Mr. and Mrs. Diosdado never told him was that the apartment was actually theirs; they had bought it months before he started college and it was meant to be part of his inheritance. The monthly "rent" was paid directly to Mr. and Mrs. Diosdado, because according to them, they did not want Dionisio to bother the old lady; this money was part of what his parents gave him every month as a stipend.

Despite his weak physical heart, Dionisio decided to formally exercise for the first time in his life, not really to get buffed up, but at least to provide some definition to his inconspicuous muscles. One day, glancing at the bulletin board at the university, he found a piece of paper indicating inexpensive tennis lessons. What was interesting about these lessons was the instructor: Claudia Berea. She was a small, thin girl with a body wanting to develop a little more and with no indication of being a tennis player, much less a tennis instructor. Claudia Berea was Dionisio's calculous classmate, where she showed an enviable intellect that allow her to derivate and integrate any equation without problems. Dionisio and La Berea, as he called her, sat close to each other during class. They initially talked about classes, calculous problems, and sometimes about other classmates. When Dionisio found out that La Berea was the tennis instructor, he asked her about potential days to practice and the price per lesson. She told him that her schedule was not busy because he was the first one to inquire about her services. They decided to practice on Tuesdays at seven in the morning, the day that their classes did not start until eleven. La Berea arrived to the first lesson dressed as a professional: all white, mini skirt, hair in a ponytail, short socks and tennis shoes that looked recently purchased for the occasion. She brought with her a basket with at least one hundred brand new green tennis balls and a pair of rackets in their sleeves. In contrast, Dionisio arrived with the first clothes he found in his closet: a green t-shirt, short denim pants, white socks, and a very worn-out pair of sneakers. He borrowed a wood racket from his parents' house that was as heavy as a cross. La Berea kept any comment about Dionisio's attire to herself and decided not to laugh until the first lesson was over. Dionisio asked her to go easy on him because he didn't want his heart to overwork. La Berea thought that he was joking and made him work and run as if in boot-camp. *Where does this tiny woman get all this stamina?* Dionisio asked himself as he tried to catch his breath and his cardiac rhythm. The next day, every single muscle in Dionisio's body hurt, while La Berea seemed as fresh as a lettuce. La Berea asked him how he was feeling. He did not answer.

Despite starting the lessons on the wrong foot, Dionisio continued with their sessions. He liked that he was learning something new and as time passed, he made significant progress in a sport he had never played before. Playing tennis also provided him with energy and helped him to be more alert in classes, as well as providing a boost when he delivered pizzas at night. His heart seemed to agree with the exercise, his episodes were nowhere to be seen and The Death was far away. But also, he enjoyed La Berea's company. She became a good friend and a confidant. La Berea felt comfortable with him as well, and she told him many aspects of her life, including how sad she was since her high school sweetheart moved to the capital to study, and that he did not visit her very often.

One Tuesday, when schools were suspended due to a faculty strike that lasted a couple of days, Dionisio invited La Berea to have a coffee in his apartment after the tennis lesson. La Berea accepted the invitation, but indicated that she preferred to take a shower first, and Dionisio, just to be nice, told her that she could shower at his apartment. To his surprise, La Berea accepted. As if she were at her own house, La Berea went directly to the shower while Dionisio prepared the coffee. When he was in the middle of grinding the coffee beans, Dionisio heard that La Berea was calling him, asking him for the soap. Dionisio got close to the bathroom door and told her the soap was in a drawer beside the sink. La Berea answered that she did not want to get cold and asked him if it was not too much trouble to come inside and give it to her. Dionisio obeyed without saying a word, entered the bathroom, got a new soap, unwrapped, it and extended his hand pushing the shower curtain just a bit, avoiding at all times peeking at something he should not. La Berea grabbed the soap, gave thanks, and started a small conversation with Dionisio. He, which was indeed focused on the conversation, did not realize that La Berea had finished her shower and came out from inside the curtain. La Berea's body was beautiful, almost like a child's, and her skin was smooth and perfect with the cinnamon tone characteristic of people from La Costa. La Berea said nothing when she realized that Dionisio was staring at her naked body like an idiot and proceed to dry herself and dress in front of him.

The tennis lessons continued and extended to Saturday mornings, when they would go back to Dionisio's apartment to drink coffee, eat bread, and for La Berea to take a quick shower. Dionisio would get into the bathroom to chat with her and sometimes he would open the curtain to have a better conversation with her, but in reality, he just wanted to watch her shower. This ritual happened for many weeks. One Saturday, La Berea asked Dionisio is he wanted to shower with her, to which he answered *no*, because the shower was too small for two people, but instead Dionisio asked her if she needed help drying herself. La Berea thought this petition was weird, but accepted. Dionisio took a towel and paced it over her body, less concerned about drying her than to enjoy the moment. When he passed the towel on her butt, La Berea stopped him and told him that if he was going to touch her behind, he'd better do it like a real man. Dionisio did not know how a real man would grab a woman's behind and decided to squeeze it hard; La Barea responded with a soft moan. Dionisio left her breasts for the end, and when he was ready to proceed, La Berea told him that if he touched them, he would have to make love to her. Dionisio nodded like a small kid. In reality, Dionisio was shaking and had no idea how to proceed; it was the first time that he was in such a situation, and despite that he had imagined it many times since he saw her naked for the first time, the reality was intensely scary. He hugged her and kissed her with more fear than passion. She loosened herself from his arms and instead jumped on him to hug him with her naked legs causing him to lose his foot falling hard on the bathroom floor. It was a hard hit but he pretended to be ok. With a hurt behind, Dionisio made love for the first time to a woman. It was nothing special, no fireworks, but he liked it. La Berea was not a bad lover, and it seemed that she had done it many times previously, most likely with the far away boyfriend; but he never knew because he never gathered the courage to asked her. The Saturday tennis lessons and the sex became a routine, but as time passed, Dionisio's tolerance towards La Berea decreased. He did not understand why, he simply started to dislike her. One day, while drinking their coffee, La Berea threw at him an 'I love you', so defined and certain that it perforated Dionisio's heart. He thought about Paola and what he said to her. He did it again: "But I don't."

That was the end of their relationship. They never talked to each other again despite being in the same classes. La Berea resumed the relationship with her high school sweetheart, who several years later died unexpectedly in a car accident.

"You have a really bad heart."

"Are you serious? I've known this since I was a little kid."

"I am not talking about your physical heart. You haven't treated women with respect, you humiliate them especially when they are falling for you."

Dionisio did not answer, but Claudia's comment bothered him.

"I touched a nerve, didn't I?" said Claudia proudly, but with some sadness.

There was no response. Claudia hesitated before asking something else.

"Do you love me?"

"Only because you aren't mine." he smiled while answering.

"And that makes you happy?"

Dionisio said no more, but she could read his answer on his face.

After Claudia Berea there were more women. Once he started having feelings for them, he would discard them as if they were disposable. He entered a vicious cycle that he enjoyed, but rarely satisfied him. Those were the days that a dream became recurrent in Dionisio's conscience, a dream that would follow him until the day he died: a large meadow covered by falling snow and in the middle of it, a large dark brown buffalo. Sometimes, in the same meadow, he would see a woman's face that seemed familiar to him: maybe it was The Death, but of this, he was not certain.

He spent his last year of college in solitude, basically interacting just with very few acquaintances. His only refuge was Veronica Bunje.

Veronica Bunje, or *Verunje*, as she was called by the students in college, was a physiology professor of around fifty years old. Verunje came from a small town in Romania, barely visible in most maps. Her parents escaped the communist regime that persecuted any person that looked suspicious of being a traitor. The Bunjes departed with Veronica in their arms and the few personal belongings they had. Destiny decided that the Bunjes would end up in La Costa, where they had no other option but to work hard to survive. After much effort, Verunje's parents had enough money to send their daughter to school and college. She became a doctor in Salamanca and also married one, and together they had a couple of boys. As her parents aged, she quit her job moved back to La Costa to dedicate all the time to her parents' care while they were thinking to die or not, something that they were very reluctant to do. But they finally died, and Verunje ended up with no job and zero activities to do. Her husband, who moved a few months to La Costa after her and quickly found a job as an internist, saw the sadness and borderline depression his wife was experiencing. He found out through a friend that the university at La Costa had an open position for a full-time professor in physiology. He mentioned it to Verunje, who without hesitation, the very next day, was in the Dean's office selling all her academic virtues. She was hired on the spot.

Verunje was a tall woman with an accentuated figure, she had a round face like a good Eastern European, auburn hair, and with the strange peculiarity of having one green and one blue eye, which made everybody look at her twice. Her students were terrified of her because she was usually in a terrible mood, she was very strict during her lectures and the ignorance of her students drove her insane. She would give the students tests that nobody was able to pass: her questions were not only complicated, they were borderline esoteric. Dionisio detested her class because he felt that he was not learning a thing from this crazy woman. In her class, Dionisio obtained the worst grade in a test during his college years: out of 100 points, he got 10. The same day he received this awful grade, Dionisio full of anger, went directly to her office to complain about the test. She greeted him calmly and with a smile, and with an attitude that was one hundred and eighty degrees different from what he had seen of her.

Despite her attitude, Dionisio complained firmly and went on a lengthy tangent about how unjust her test was and told her that her questions were unintelligible. Verunje listened to him patiently, sometimes she would smile with sympathy or nod in agreement. After Dionisio ended his rant, Veronica Bunje explained to him that he should not worry much about the test and his horrific grade; she mentioned that most students had a similar grade and at the end she was going to curve the grade. This calmed Dionisio a little. Verunje then changed the topic and started talking about things Dionisio considered irrelevant. He answered her with monosyllabic responses because he did not want to stay there longer that what was needed. Verunje noticed his urgency and let him go, but when he opened the office door, Verunje asked him if he could come the to her office after the next class. Dionisio agreed without knowing why.

Dionisio sat down to chat with Verunje for more time than he would have imagined. Verunje would chat about her parents, their troubles, and how they managed to escape from the old Romania, about her kids, husband, and love, and admiration for the Pope, that according to her, was the only one that fought hard to end the communistic regime in her old country. At the beginning, Dionisio listened to her because he had to, but eventually he learned to appreciate her conversations. Verunje looked at him as if he were her son and sometimes she would get close to him to caress his hair or give him a lateral hug. One day, Verunje asked him if he had a car, Dionisio answered that he had a very old one he used to deliver pizzas, but rarely drove it anywhere else. She followed that question by asking him whether he wanted a ride home. He thought of that offer as a little weird, but gladly accepted it. That started a small ritual of leaving together. One December night, when it was already dark, they found themselves outside Dionisio's apartment complex, with the security post being the only visible light. They were talking about anything until they suddenly realized that the air inside the car had become electrified. Dionisio, with intention, crossed his left hand to Verunje's seat to touch her leg. She felt him and without any warning, she threw herself at him to give him a succulent kiss on the lips, and then she whispered in his ear saying that they could be the greatest lovers this earth would ever see. This comment scared Dionisio to the bone.

He was not mistaken to be afraid. Veronica Bunje was a sexual tornado, much more than Dionisio could handle. He concluded that either Verunje was a sex professional, a nymphomaniac, or just plain insane. Although Dionisio learned and enjoyed a lot through his sexual adventures with Verunje, what was more fulfilling to him was her friendship. Dionisio opened to her as he had never done with anyone before, and he told her everything about him including about his weak heart and The Death that was constantly around him. Verunje would look at him intensely with her bicolor eyes, probably trying to psychoanalyze him.

"Forget about women," Verunje told him while naked on Dionisio's bed, "think about yourself. It's obvious that you are of no use to them and they are useless to you."

"What about you? I'm here for you." Dionisio answered with some resentment.

"I am not here for you and you are not here for me. Since the moment we met, we knew that this relationship would be short lived. You are here for yourself and I am here for myself. The rest doesn't matter. Whatever we have between us is just a mere distraction. Look, sometimes the love for oneself is the best lover one can ever find. There are times that I am driving alone and I want to love myself as if it were the last day on earth. So, I pull over in an empty street, close my eyes and imagine what I would want the most in that instant, and if I need to satisfy myself, I do, and I enjoy it as if it were the first time.

"Satisfy yourself?" asked Dionisio, with little pleasure. It was true, he regarded the act of satisfying oneself to be animalistic.

"Yes and no; sex constitutes a small part about relationships. One can live happily without the need of falling in love with another person. And if one likes to satisfy oneself, great."

"How can you say all this when you have been married for so many years, and it seems you love your husband?"

"My marriage could exist or not, and I would be as happy either way. My sentimental life is complete with me, the rest is just an ornament. I love him, but he does not complete me or define me. I am me, and that is enough."

"I don't think so."

"It is fine if you don't believe me today, but one day you will realize that you are the only one needed for your happiness, and that you would do anything to be happy;" Verunje stopped for a second to see the face of that young man that looked at her as if he had fallen in love. "And I say this to you so that we do not have misunderstandings: Dionisio, I do not love you and you do not love me. This friendship or peculiar relationship is just physical and with some Oedipus in it. We will never fall in love because we both know that because of obvious reasons, I will not leave my husband or my family for a young and inexperienced man. And you will not want to live with a woman that in ten years would be around sixty, with withered skin. Look, one day I will get tired of you and when that happens, I will dump you in an instant."

Verunje ended her prophetic sermon, held his hand and dragged him on top of her to make love one more time. Dionisio, that looked to her as a weird version of a mother, respected whatever she said, and had no other option but to say yes to wha she said.

That night, sleep came difficult to Dionisio because Verunje's words circulated in his mind. When he finally fell asleep, Dionisio dreamed that his heart was flying over oceans, deserts, mountains, trying to find a place to rest. And after circling the earth, it finally landed under Dionisio's ribs. He woke up, went to the restroom and when he looked at his reflection in the mirror, the reflection did not recognize the person on the other side.

A few months later, at the end of the school day, Dionisio walked to Veronica Bunje's office as he had done many times before. The light inside the office was on as a signal that she was inside. When he tried to open the door, he found it locked. Dionisio knocked a couple of times without getting an answer, and when he was ready to knock again, he found a small envelop attached to the door's frame. The envelop was addressed to Dionisio Diosdado. He took it and from the inside he retrieved a small letter. The writing was brief: "Today is the day. Have an incredible life. And remember, you are the only one that will make you happy, VB." Dionisio froze in place, staring at the door. The only thing that crossed his mind was "thank you."

"And you have not seen her?"

"I tried one day, I went to the university and knocked on her door. She opened as if she were waiting for me. She greeted me amicably and asked me what she could do for me. I told her that I wanted to talk, tell each other our lives, catch up. Verunje smiled and told me she couldn't, and the same way she greeted me she said goodbye. Somehow, she erased me from her life."

"Have you erased her from yours?" Asked Claudia.

"I have never cried for her. It was like a contract had expired. But I have not erased her."

Part 14

Claudia and Dionisio met in November. At the beginning, their relationship was limited to meetings at the bridge. Their chats followed a regular course, they would chat about their lives, the weather, favorite movies, and such topics. But after the episode when Claudia listened to his heart, or hers, who knows, beating inside his chest, the conversation limits expanded. Both would stand at the bridge to watch the sea while they talked, or sometimes they just remained quiet thinking about each other. Dionisio would stand very close to Claudia to pretend accidental touches on her leg with his hand. Claudia would not complain.

"Let's go to the Café del Mar." Dionisio asked abruptly.

"That is a couples' restaurant." answered Claudia.

"I know, but it is a very nice place."

"What about Juan Carlos?"

"What about him?"

"He is my fiancé and I cannot go out with anyone to a romantic place like that one; it's not appropriate."

"I am not just anyone, right?"

"Don't be stupid, I don't mean it like that. The point is that I cannot."

"Ok then, come with me to the beach to have a coffee at Puerto. That place is not romantic at all."

Claudia thought briefly. She knew it was not appropriate to go out for a coffee with another man when she was engaged, however the idea seemed very intriguing.

"I don't know, I need to talk with Juan Carlos to see if he's ok with it."

"Wow! I don't think he's going to give you permission." mocked Dionisio.

Dionisio was incorrect about Juan Carlos: he did not give much importance about Claudia having a coffee with one of her friends, on the contrary, Juan Carlos thought it was a great idea.

Before ending college, Juan Carlos had already been offered a good job position aligned at the El Negro Legorrea's firm in La Costa. It was a good opportunity for him in the area of criminology that he loved much, and the salary was not bad for a junior associate. They even gave him the opportunity to take time off between college and the starting date, which he accepted and took a year off. On top of that, the idea of living close to the beach was for him, fantastic. The day that Juan Carlos mentioned to Claudia about the offer in La Costa, that very same day, he proposed to her telling Claudia that he would not be able to live in La Costa without her. For her, that was not a difficult decision, she knew that Juan Carlos was the man of her life and she loved him dearly. She happily said yes to the marriage proposal, but asked him to first live together to make sure they could adapt as a couple. Claudia moved with him to La Costa and it did not take much time before she found her job as a data analyst in a chemical company dedicated to the production of plastics and their derivatives. The change of scenery was good for Claudia, with the exception that it became somewhat difficult for her to establish relationships in her new city.

Claudia would mention Dionisio to Juan Carlos, but her fiancé did not pay much attention to that. He thought that Dionisio was, according to what he could gather from Claudia, not really an excellent person but at least a nice one. It was clear that Claudia would tell him only the things that she considered appropriate, the rest she would keep them to herself with a grain of culpability.

It was late and the sun wanted to set to let the dusk lay over the beach. It was the beginning of the year, but the day was warm and humid. Very few people were at the beach that evening, some were running and others were laying on towels trying to soak up the last sunrays of the day. The two of them decided to take their shoes off to feel the still warm sand under their naked feet, and sometimes they would walk close to the edge between the ocean and the beach to feel the water. The café Puerto was still far away, but they were able to see it at the distance, although by the way they were walking, any passerby would have assumed they were in no rush to get anywhere. They walked like people that have known each other for a long time and felt very comfortable with each other's presence. The sun finally set behind the mountain range, leaving both walkers illuminated by the lamps on the side of the street. It was at that moment that a strange sensation dawned upon Claudia and Dionisio making them stop. It was like an invisible cloud covered them in something difficult to describe. As a reflex, Dionisio took Claudia's hand and when she felt him, she held him firmly. Time is relative, and it depends on the speed at which one is traveling, sometimes the world passes really fast and sometimes it crawls. Their minds, their hearts, even Dionisio's ill one, their blood, their thoughts, their hormones, all turned into particles traveling trajectories at light speed, causing everything around them to move agonizingly slow. Dionisio and Claudia, Claudia and Dionisio. It was not an agony for them; on the contrary, they felt that what was lacking in them, that joy that one carries hidden inside and that only true beauty, such as the sun rising or the smile of a baby can bring to the surface, appeared and completed them. Maybe, just maybe, they felt true happiness. But true happiness is not stable in this world, like a rare element that lives only for a few seconds because even the air is against it. And in the same way it appeared, it vanished, without notice or promise to come back, leaving Claudia Alicante and Dionisio Diosdado like columns stuck in the lukewarm sand. They were holding hands, holding their shoes with the other hand, with their souls wrapped in each other, but with their minds completely foggy.

They arrived to café Puerto with little to say, like zombies. They sat at the first table they found available and ordered a drink: Claudia a margarita and Dionisio a strong coffee. They were trying to avoid each other's eyes, and the atmosphere, as if a vacuum had sucked up all the good particles, turned stagnant and sour. The only thing they would eventually remember about that evening was that

Claudia, for the first time since her college years, had alcohol.

On his way back, Dionisio was scared and scattered, his mind was completely blank. No thoughts reached his mind and he perceived a terrifying mental void. Instead of going home, he decided to go to work which sounded more reassuring than his own place. He was there past midnight and when he was almost falling asleep, he finally went home. He could feel Her presence in the car, he did not want to use the mirror, afraid of finding Her in the back seat. And he was right, there in the back seat, sitting like a good girl, was The Death, taking a ride with Dionisio.

Before falling asleep for the short January night ahead of him, Dionisio's mind travelled throughout the endless corners of his memory. He found Ena, Paola, and many more women he had met, but the memory of them was not pleasant; they were people that wanted to hurt him. He found himself being embarrassed one more time by Ena, being marked by her for life. He found himself dreaming about this memory, recreated over and over in his mind, maybe adding new details, tainting it. A memory that Dionisio transformed anyway he wanted; a quasi-false memory that became a story that he would tell with extreme detail, first to Verunje and then to Claudia. A tale that entered Claudia's mind as a fact and made her feel some mercy for that man. It was not a lie, it was the truth, his truth, impure, massaged, transformed.

That night, in his dream, he realized that he loved Claudia, maybe with some obsession. But instead of being comforted by this thought, he felt terrified. He also thought that Claudia loved him too, increasing his horror. He felt suffocated and wanted to escape his dream. He woke up and his mind raced. The sunlight started to creep through the windows of his room, and inside of him he realized that he could not have any type of relationship with Claudia. But she was still inside of him, like a presence bouncing in his mind and thoughts, destroying everything inside, causing chaos. A presence that never went away, and stayed with him even until his last breath in that cold hospital bed in Salamanca where he heard for the last time that woman's voice. Claudia was a mental storm.

Claudia went back to her house. Once inside, she kissed her hellos with Juan Carlos, she quickly answered a few of his questions and then went to bed. It was hard for her to fall asleep. She did not dream, but when she woke up, there were no doubts in her mind.

Part 15

Dionisio did not go back to the bridge to avoid meeting with her, and instead had lunch in his office. He put extra energy and hours into his work, he spent long days analyzing results and projects. He became even quieter, barely talking to his co-workers, primarily focusing on his work, which he found helpful to keep his mind occupied. But at night, those were hours that pounded and punished him with images of Claudia. He would think about conversations with her where he would ask her many questions to which he already knew how she would respond. In his mind, Claudia was dressed with different clothing of various colors; there, he could approach her freely, touching her exposed skin that the clothes allowed to show, he felt her little hairs on her arms, neck. He could breathe in her scent. He then further extended his working hours to avoid meeting her in his mind. He would stay at work past midnight and head home each night mortally tired, allowing him to fall asleep as soon as he touched his pillow. He would wake up very early, take a shower, dress, eat something for breakfast, and prepare his lunch. During the weekends, Dionisio would escape to his parent's house; Mr. and Mrs. Diosdado loved having their only child with them. He would talk with his father about planes, about life, and would help him fix whatever was needed at home. It was then that Dionisio found out that the apartment belonged to his parents, and never to an old lady, and that it would be part of his inheritance. Dionisio was surprised, in a very positive manner, that his parents came up with the story of the old lady; he laughed with his dad and at himself. Dionisio asked his dad to please keep accepting the little money he paid for rent. Mr. Diosdado gladly agreed. At his parents' home, his mom would cook for him his favorite dishes, curries, meat with spicy sauces, fried plantains. She would always cook an extra portion for Dionisio to take home and have something for the work week. He rediscovered his love for his parents. His mind rested for a season. But he never mentioned to them anything about Claudia.

Claudia understood the last evening she saw Dionisio that he was the man she had been looking for all her life. The feeling she had for that man had grown and she needed to see him, talk to him, have him, possess him as he possessed her. In Claudia's mind, she wanted him to pursue her, make him chase her and free her from whatever was trapping her. Claudia knew with certainty that she was engraved in his mind, too. But what to do with Juan Carlos? She did not want to break his heart; she still loved him. She played the love game with Juan Carlos; they

went often to the movies or out to eat, and in one of
those occasions, in the form of a rushed comment,
Claudia asked him when they would get married. She
thought that question was going to scare him since
they were happily living together with no legal
commitment, she was hoping for a fight. The plan
backfired when he told her that they should plan the
wedding for December of that year. She was cornered
and did not know what to do. She spent the following
weeks looking for dresses and wedding packages. To
her surprise, she found herself enjoying preparing for
the wedding because in her mind, she would see
herself marrying Dionisio. *Am I being fair to Juan
Carlos?* she asked herself one day while they were
having dinner. Her answered scared her; she stood
up from the table abruptly and without notice left to
the restroom. She locked herself in and when she
saw her reflection in the mirror, she could not find the
Claudia of her childhood, the little one crying over her
parents' death, the one that lived under the shadows
of her grandparents, the young girl studying in
Salamanca. Instead, she saw in the mirror the
reflection of Ena, a young girl she never met but
imagined clearly in her mind. She thought that she
was going crazy and fell on to the floor to cry silent,
sour tears. Outside the bathroom, Juan Carlos was
waiting for her, concerned.

Part 16

Summer brought with itself a terrible heat wave
that basically pasteurized everything in La Costa. It
was exhausting to get out to the street under that
July's sun, baking every single person that didn't have
the time to go to the beach to refresh or that simply
did not enjoy Summer's warmth. Dionisio was one of

them. To him, the heat and humidity of La Costa were unbearable. As he grew older, he tolerated the Summers less. On top of that, the number of insects and flying organisms that basked in the heat increased exponentially. Spiders, as a consequence of the increment of insects and other pests, would come out from their hiding nooks and make their webs in every conceivable corner. The more insects they caught, the more they grew, creating pests of Biblical proportions. Dionisio hated them and all insects and other bugs, especially those with wings that could whoosh over his ears; to him these animals were simply Nature's mistakes. Getting out of his house during the summer months was a sacrifice he tried to avoid as much as possible. On one of those inevitable days when the temperature was around 40 degrees Celsius, he ventured out of the office to have a snack, and when he got into the elevator, he found himself alone with Claudia. When she saw her, she was in so much shock that it seemed as if she had seen a spirit. Both were courteous and greeted each other in a hurry. It was obvious that the air in the elevator had filled with the particles that make people feel awkward. Claudia danced almost imperceptibly on her feet. Dionisio started sweating and felt his heart of flesh beating erratically; he felt chills running throughout his skin and his sweat turned ice cold. He turned pale. Claudia asked him if he was feeling well to which he answered honestly and said *No*. They got off the elevator and Claudia dragged him to a close by bench. She sat him down carefully and with a magazine that was already on the bench, she fanned his face.

"Is it your heart?"

"Yes, it is bothering me. It's being a while since I had one of these episodes."

"Dionisio, I know the doctors haven't been too useful, but I think you should go and see another one. Maybe there is a new therapy or medication on the market that may help you. Would you promise me that you'll go see the doctor?"

Dionisio did not answer.

"Do you want something to drink? Water, soda?" said Claudia with a lot of care.

"No, thanks. It'll go away."

Silence, and both still felt uncomfortable. Finally, Dionisio broke the awkwardness.

"You don't have to stay with me. You may be in a rush or late for something."

"I'm in no hurry, and I would like to stay with you until you feel well enough, if that is OK with you?"

"That's fine."

Silence.

"Claudia, this may sound weird, but thanks for being here with me. It's comforting to know that you were the one close by when the episode happened."

Claudia smiled.

"How are you feeling?" asked Claudia, knowing the answer.

"Still bad, but at least I am not getting worse…since we are here, tell me about your life."

"You already know a lot about my life, maybe more than what you should." answered Claudia, somewhat serious.

"No, I mean, what have you done in the past few months?"

Conflicted, Claudia answered him that she was happy, planning her wedding with Juan Carlos. She did not elaborate much and Dionisio only nodded in response.

"And, what about you?" asked Claudia, as if she were daring him to one-up her answer.

"Nothing, here…still alive."

Claudia looked at him and saw a man that was aging rapidly or may be a man that had lost something in his life: his eyes reflected a lack of hope, they looked scattered. But also, for an instant, she saw herself in his eyes. She loved him there even more. On the other hand, Dionisio saw her eyes and found himself cursed, not because Claudia was a bad omen, but because he saw the woman he loved but had no intention of letting her know. His soul hurt. He pretended to be better, stood up, said thank you and goodbye, and left quickly to the elevator that with one ding had just announced its arrival.

Claudia left the building worried about Dionisio. She decided to call him the next day at his office, and without thinking twice, she did it. Dionisio answered and was surprised to hear Claudia's voice on the other side. They gave each other the mandatory greetings and Claudia asked him how he was feeling. He told her that once he went back to his office, he felt much better, and that the episode was long gone. Dionisio, that was in an uncommonly good mood, told Claudia that after the episode, he left work much earlier than usual, and while he was walking on the street to the parking lot, two very strange things happened to him: the first one was about an old lady that approached him, thinking that he was Enrique Balboa, and before Dionisio could have corrected her, the lady proceed with a ten-minute monologue about her life, which frankly was very interesting and made Dionisio really pay attention to her. The old lady finished by telling him that he should visit her and she would prepare that delicious coconut dessert he liked so much. Dionisio decided not to correct or disappoint the old lady, and told her that he would try to visit her soon. Once they said their goodbyes, the second strange thing happened: he walked two steps and he felt something hitting his cheek, followed by feeling wet. It took him a few seconds to react. He turned his head and saw a car speeding up with several teenager heads staring at him. On the sidewalk, he found the deflated remains of a blue balloon. Dionisio connected the dots and concluded that those good-for-nothing teens threw a water balloon at him. He was furious, but at the same time, the water was refreshing. On the other side of the telephone Claudia was laughing out loud.

"Why are you laughing?"

"Because those two things that happened to you are very funny. And the way you tell them is incredible. You know how to tell stories!"

"You wouldn't be laughing if this had happened to you."

They ended their conversation and Claudia realized that she missed that man's presence, his anecdotes, and stories of his life. She knew she was lacking something, and instead of feeling sad, she grabbed the phone and called him again to ask if he wanted to go out to lunch soon. Dionisio was even more surprised from the second phone call and invitation, but without hesitation he said yes.

That night, Claudia's mind traveled to places where she had not been in a long time. She felt comfortable with Dionisio in her mind. She thought about Juan Carlos, but his image was unfamiliar and distant.

That same night, Dionisio dreamed with Claudia's silhouette laying on his bed. The room was dark and the rain was falling hard on the street below. Claudia's back was facing him and only her subtle breathing movements were noticeable. Dionisio got closer to see her and touch her naked back that was uncovered by the bed sheets. When he was about to touch her, he stopped and instead sat by her side. He did not notice it at the beginning, but now he could see that on the other side of the bed there was a mirror softly reflecting the dark room. In that mirror, he noticed two small slits projecting a yellow light. Dionisio jumped; those were Claudia's eyes, diabolic and horrendous. With otherworldly telepathy, the eye forced Dionisio to look at Claudia's naked back: on it he saw his life line, the same one that Magdalena had read many years ago on his palm. Similar to the life line on his hand, the one on Claudia's back also formed and eye, and eye of different colors, like Verunje's eyes. Dionisio woke up abruptly and immediately looked at his palm: there, the eye was boldly looking at him.

Part 17

There are few people with the right vision to start a business and to make it a success, especially a restaurant. Fernando Viruega was one of those individuals. People called him The Priest of La Costa, only because he enjoyed having discussions about religion, of any kind. When he was young and broke, The Priest only had enough money to buy almost spoiled chicken thighs that he would prepare with regular mustard and sometimes ketchup, ending up with a dish that was borderline disgusting. He reached a point in which his chicken dish became simply a way to introduce a few nutrients into his body, and at this point he decided that he could do better. He saved money to save for some spices and when he gathered a good collection of them he combined them in different proportions to marinate the chicken. After many trials and an equal number of failures, he found a recipe that was not only excellent to the palate, but also with a good degree of spiciness. What brought his dish to the next level was that he deep-fried the chicken. That was how The Priest concocted the best spicy fried chicken in La Costa, and in many other cites, that in collaboration with beans, rice, and fried plantains, created a piece of heaven on earth. He opened a small business that grew exponentially once a local news reporter interviewed him as part of an "Eat with the locals" series. The very next day after the show aired, a large line was seen outside the business, which was unofficially named, *The Pollo Priest*.

Claudia had heard about The Pollo Priest and was very curious to try it. The restaurant was halfway between her house and work, off La Principal, and she always noticed on her way back home a considerable amount of people outside forming a line. She mentioned to Juan Carlos about the restaurant and that she really wanted to try it. Juan Carlos was not a fan of trying new things, especially related to food, and The Pollo Priest, according to Juan Carlos, did not look like a trustworthy establishment, despite the enormous fame it had earned. But he went with her, and he hated it: the chicken was to greasy for his taste and extremely spicy for his tender lips and tongue. Claudia, on the other hand, thought that the chicken was the best dish she had ever tried in La Costa. Both of them, however, woke up the next day with an unmerciful watery diarrhea. Juan Carlos swore not to step foot again in The Pollo Priest, whereas Claudia tried to go there at least once a month. Eventually, her gastrointestinal system got used to the spicy chicken and the diarrhea disappeared after a few more visits. Every time she entered the restaurant, The Priest would greet her by name and complement her politely about her appearance. He was pleased that 'the boyfriend' did not come with her anymore and one day he told her that 'that guy is not for you.' She ignored the comment, but that evening she thought about it for a long time.

"You want to have lunch at The Pollo Priest?" Dionisio asked.

"Yes, it is the best in La Costa."

"Sure, the best if you want to get diarrhea or a good gastric ulcer. And, it is far away from work, we cannot walk there."

"We'll drive. C'mon, you are going to like it. I cannot imagine that you have never been there!"

"I am already sick of my heart, I do not want to destroy my intestines…but sure, let's go."

Claudia and Dionisio arranged to meet at the parking lot where Claudia parked her car. At the beginning, the conversation was scarce because both of them felt foreign; the break they had from each other removed part of their closeness. Eventually the conversation picked up, first about the chicken, then about the weather and finally about Juan Carlos and Claudia's upcoming wedding. Dionisio watched Claudia with emphasis, he watched her mouth movements, her thin lips that every-now-and-then her tongue would moisten, the whiteness of her teeth and the words that came out of her mouth. Claudia monopolized the conversation; it was clear that she had started to feel very comfortable. Dionisio would just answer with short pre-made phrases and sometimes he would present his opinion.

When they arrived at The Pollo Priest, the line was long; they waited close to 20 minutes to be at the front. Claudia greeted The Priest with enthusiasm and in the same mood introduced him to Dionisio. The Priest studied him and then got close to Claudia's ear to let her know in a whisper that this boy, despite being small, ugly, and with a tadpole face, was a keeper. Claudia enjoyed The Priest's wisdom, but did not answer when Dionisio asked her what that was all about.

Dionisio tried the chicken with caution, but after the first bite he realized he was eating mana from heaven. Maybe it was the spiciness working as a stimulant that resulted in Dionisio talking freely to Claudia about his life, in such an entertaining and funny way that Claudia was simply mesmerized. Claudia watched Dionisio intensely, she watched his thin mouth, his not-very-white teeth, his lips that opened and closed to let the words play with the imagination for her to feel that it was herself actually living Dionisio's anecdotes. Suddenly, she wanted to kiss him, she thought about getting close and fusing her lips with his, but she did not do it.

They left The Pollo Priest and happily started on their way back to work. When they were in the elevator, Claudia got close to him to say goodbye: she kissed him on the cheek, a three-quarters kiss that touched enough of the lips' edge to feel moist and left her with a wonderful flavor that accompanied her all day long.

Part 18

Claudia's dreams turned into a mixture of guilt and lust. Dionisio was in most them showing her all that she had never seen. There, Dionisio would talk to her, love her, she would become one with him, sometimes she would become him and live her life as his. She would turn into this small and insignificant child that dreamed about kissing Ena but only obtained her rejection. She would also turn into a late teenager experimenting a relationship with Verunje. But then, she would wake up to find Juan Carlos' silhouette, reminding her of the Claudia that she used to be. She felt ashamed and avoided to look Juan Carlos in the eyes. She pretended to love him, she forced herself to care for him all day long, but at the end, when her head hit the pillow, she would travel to the parallel universe in her dreams where she had found the man she truly wanted. She kept organizing the wedding, but now it resulted in being a chore, a task that she did not want to complete.

Claudia talked to Dionisio one more time; she told him about how great a time she had had at The Pollo Priest and told him that they should go back. Dionisio hesitated but at the end he agreed. Thus, a new Thursday routine started. Sometimes Dionisio would drive to The Pollo Priest, sometimes Claudia did.

"This chicken is so spicy that I cannot feel my lips, I think the spiciness destroyed them." said Claudia.

"Me too, I do not feel my lips and I am very dizzy. What in the world is that spiciness? What kind of evil pepper is used, or maybe it's just plain sulfuric acid."

"You are silly, but seriously, I cannot feel my lips."

"Let me touch them."
Dionisio passed his finger on Claudia's lips, feeling her flesh.

"Nothing, they are completely numbed."

"Well, wake them up by kissing me on the cheek," said Dionisio as if it were the normal thing to say in that situation.

Claudia looked at him for a second and without answering, she kissed him on the cheek. A normal kiss like the one a mother gives to her child.

"What kind of kiss was that, am I your uncle?" Dionisio responded, "come and give me a good kiss so your lips can wake up."

"That was a good kiss."

"Not at all! Come, I will show you."

"Are you going to teach me how to kiss? Please, I can lecture you about it."

"Well, if you are *that* good, show me."

Claudia held his head and kissed him on the cheeks with a similar kiss.

"That was the same kiss, you changed nothing. Look, pay attention and take notes. Put your lips apart, wet them with your tongue and then get them close to my cheek. Once you make contact, stay like that for a few seconds and end with a *mwah*. Like this."

Dionisio did exactly what he said. She received the kiss and loved the sensation. As if they were playing, Claudia told him that it was her turn and kissed him following his instructions.

"You are a great learner, most likely because you have a great teacher."

"You are really something."

That day they returned to work after lunch and when they said their goodbyes, Dionisio asked Claudia to kiss him the way he taught her. Claudia, without saying a word, obediently kissed him. Both returned to their jobs smiling.

Part 19

The Saturday afternoon that Claudia and Juan Carlos decided to go shopping for a wedding cake, a strong downpour attacked La Costa with all its fury, causing zero visibility in all the city from the northwest mountain range to the ocean. Juan Carlos was driving carefully because he could not see much of the road ahead while Claudia was on her seat almost in a fetal position trying to hide from the storm. The rain hammered the roof of the car mercilessly while monopolizing all of the sound inside the car.

"Tell me if I am getting too close to the car in front of me," asked a determined Juan Carlos to a Claudia that heard nothing but the rain mixed with her own fear. Juan Carlos repeated himself without any response from her part. The third time he did it, his voice was so loud that it deafened the rain hitting the car. Claudia jumped as she was startled, turned around to look at him with not very friendly eyes, and told him that he did not have to yell at her.

"How I am not going to yell if you do not hear me?" answered Juan Carlos.

"Well I did not hear you," she said.

"Of course, you didn't because you are there, embracing yourself like a fearful child, and afraid of what? A little, harmless storm? What could possibly go wrong?" He stopped talking, realizing the enormity of his comments, he knew quite well that Claudia's parents died in a storm. Claudia turned herself away from him and remained like that for a long time; there was no human power that could have made her change her mind.

The storm continued for one more terrifying hour and La Cuarta had become a small river. The engine of the car stalled in the middle of the storm-made river. Inside the car, Juan Carlos and Claudia's breathing clouded the windows and the interior air turned bitter, not only because of the lack of circulation, but also because neither of the two said a word. They were there until the rain stopped and the only noise was that of the ambulances and firetruck sirens going places to rescue whoever needed it, or to search for and open the manholes clogged with all the trash carried by the storm to relieve the city of the flooding.

While they were waiting for the waters to recede and for the car to start, Claudia's mind traveled in her memories, thinking about the little time she had during her childhood with her parents and the little she truly knew them. The memory tears escaped from her and she avoided being seen by Juan Carlos, which was not too difficult because he had his head outside of the window trying to figure out whether the water level was decreasing. She also thought about how it was possible to love someone so much, like her mom and dad, when she barely knew them. *Of course, I loved them, they were my parents!* she said to herself, there was that innate universal connection that any living human with enough gray matter could recognize. Of course, the intensity of the connection was different between parents and children; sometimes it was minimal and sometimes excessive. Claudia believed that the connection she had with her parents was strictly necessary. *Not like the connection I have with Dionisio*, she said to herself, which was different, indescribable, unique, and full of love, *because yes, I believe I love him*. And when this thought finished traveling through the grooves of her mind, time stopped and the thousands and thousands of liters of water that just fell from the heavens disappeared, as if someone had removed a gigantic plug, taking with them Juan Carlos' car, Juan Carlos, the noise of the sirens and even the remaining clouds that just few minutes ago had released their fury over La Costa, leaving Claudia alone by herself in a personal limbo where reality was a confused dream in which Dionisio was the main character, and her the only spectator that whispered so softly, almost as if she did not want him to hear her that she loved him; not with the romantic love seen in the movies that delights middle school girls, but with the love that connects two people deep from the bone marrow all the way up to every single skin cell, intertwining them as if they were only one person, as if in another time, another universe, they had belonged to the same whole being, and because the randomness of the world or the capricious will of a Greek or Egyptian or Hebrew god were cruelly separated without their consent.

Claudia came back from her limbo to the inside of the car, which was already moving through less deep waters and heard Juan Carlos saying that it would be best to shop for the wedding cake on another occasion. Claudia nodded with a lazy head movement.

Part 20

Melinda Ramsden was born and raised in Oxford under the constant humidity and the grey skies. Her parents were middle class and owned a little grocery store. Melinda was not interested in becoming part of the family business; she preferred to lay down on the grass and look up to the heavens and fantasize. People thought that Melinda was not completely 'there' regarding her mental capacities, mostly because she liked to be by herself and always

stared directly at a specific point. However, Melinda
turned out to be a very intelligent woman that ended
up studying at Oxford University and graduating with
a degree in ethnological studies. *Ethnological
studies?* asked Melinda's parents, who thought that
she should have studied something different, practical
that would help her economically in the future. But
they were hopeful in the idea that Melinda, because of
her many charms, would meet a lawyer or a doctor.
The professional prince never came, instead Melinda
told her parents that she had everything planned to
migrate to warmer and more exotic latitudes to study
the societies that lived there. She thought as a good
Brit, she would end up in Asia or Africa, but because
of her grant sponsors, she traveled to South America.
With twenty-one years and her parents' chastising,
Melinda Ramsden traveled with what little she had to
the southern hemisphere. According to the
established research plan, Melinda spent two years
immersed in the lower rainforest of Ecuador,
struggling to have contact with a small tribal group
that, according to legends circulating in the region, its
members were experts at reading the stars and
forecasting events almost as accurate as
Nostradamus. After hundreds of kilometers traveled
by foot through high brush, an irrational number of
mosquito bites that more than once left her in bed
sweating out fevers and malaises, facing poisonous
snakes, and the always amicable capybara peeking
out from the swamps, Melinda reached the conclusion
that such a tribe did not exist. However, every single
person in the region promised and swore by the local
saint to her that the tribe really did exist and the only
reason she could not find it was because her Spanish
was impure. Melinda just answered that such a tribe
would not speak in Spanish but most likely a unique

and rich language that few understood. Melinda concluded that all the people in the region were either crazy or playing a really elaborate and disgusting practical joke.

After two years, Melinda stopped her research and everything related to ethnic studies and left Ecuador to travel throughout South America, spending every single cent she had. When she ran out of money, she was in Buenos Aires. She had much more fluent Spanish and started working, out of necessity, in a department store wrapping up presents. She hated the job because she thought that it was useless to wrap something when eventually it would be ripped apart and destroyed, like making the bed in the morning when at night it would just be undone. However, this job allowed her to make enough money to live and save little. After six months, she quit and bought a plane ticket and ended up in La Costa. La Costa seemed to her as an enchanting place, very different from the rest of Latin America, with a large beach with soft sands spreading along the coast for many kilometers, surrounded by the great mountain range, and full of beautiful people, as she used to call them. The first thing Melinda did was to find a place to live, which she found rather easily, but due to her economic situation the apartment she found was horrible. It was full of small white lizards and dark brown roaches of almost 5 centimeters long, and as if it were Nature's joke or curse, these horrible insects were capable of expanding their terror because they could fly. But Melinda did not care much about these pests because she'd seen worse in the lower basin of Ecuador.

She would spend hours upon hours laying on the beach; she liked to tan and stare at the horizon, thinking about the cloudy and rainy days in the Oxford of her childhood, but the sun would only turn her white skin into a shrimp-like pink that burned during the nights. In the same way that she cared little about her skin being burned by the sun, she also cared little about her economic situation. She lived with what she had saved while in Buenos Aires, and to make it last, she just had one meal per day. She lost weight, but didn't look ill.

Mr. Diosdado used to take long walks along the beach because, according to him, that was his weekly exercise that was accompanied at the end by having a good snack consisting of baked pastries painted with melted butter that a hunchback lady used to sell close to the beach. It was during one of these walks that Mr. Diosdado, when he was not paying too much attention to his surroundings, did not see Melinda laying down sunbathing, and he tripped over her. Mr. Diosdado lost his balance and ended up falling slowly over Melinda, landing most of his weight on Melinda's forearm that released a distinct cracking sound. Melinda screamed in pain and her face was full of tears; suddenly a small crowd gathered around. Mr. Diosdado, after recovering from the fall, realized what he had done and tried to soothe Melinda, with little effect. He finally convinced her to let him take her to the closest emergency room. He carefully helped her into his car, that was not far away, and then like a maniac, drove to the hospital. The result was that Melinda had a transversal fracture of the radius and needed a cast. Once the pain receded, thanks to the painkillers, and Melinda was ready to be released, Mr. Diosdado begged her to please let him take her to her house. She accepted. He walked her to her door and as she was getting into her apartment, Mr. Diosdado realized the gravity of the apartment's infestation and the extremely poor living conditions, and due to his overwhelming guilt, he asked her, mostly as a reflex, to spend some days at his house. Melinda fought the idea, but at the end she gave in, took a few of her belongings and left with him. Once Mrs. Diosdado had heard the complete story, she welcomed Melinda to her house with ease, and extended the invitation to stay with them until she was able to find a steady job and able to afford a better place for herself without lizards, flying roaches or any other pest.

Part 21

The ant was really small, those little black ones that are found sometimes walking around the kitchen as if they owned the place and ignoring the enormous black shadows that may smash them at any moment. Its size was as small as its awareness of the surroundings, walking up and down on that strange surface. It was looking for some food or for the chemical trail left by others like it; she probably wanted to go back to her anthill. Dionisio saw it and became distracted by the ant.

"Why are you looking at my legs?"

"Well, first, your legs are a luxury item, and second because you have a tiny ant walking on your thigh."

"What!! Why haven't you mentioned it before?" said Claudia, while hastily brushing the ant away with her hand.

"Why did you do that? You probably killed it."

"I'm sorry. Forget about the ant and keep telling me about Melinda."

"As I was telling you, Melinda is living now in my parent's house because they felt sorry about the conditions of her apartment. She is now living in my old room. On top of that, my dad asked me a couple of nights ago to take her out so she could be entertained and be with someone around her age. I really do not like when people are thrown at me, but since I could not think of an excuse that my dad would understand, I had to say yes."

"And where are you going to take her?"

"I don't know yet, I have a couple of days to think about it before the weekend, which is when I told my dad I will take her out. You should come with us!"

"Nah, I don't like to be involved in your things, and what if you two end up doing little things to each other?" answered Claudia with a big smile on her face.

"If that were to happen, you would be terribly jealous."

Claudia looked at him a bit upset and Dionisio felt it. He then touched her shoulder as a way to apologize, but she rejected him.

Part 22

The weekend arrived and Dionisio showed up at his parents' house as agreed. Melinda came down the stairs from his room as if she were a princess that had waited for a long time for her Prince Charming. She was dressed in a blue skirt with no intention of reaching her knees that let her thin but well-toned British legs show. She wore also a pink sleeveless top that complimented her pale skin color and matched the pink cast on her arm. Dionisio was surprised because he was not expecting Melinda to be cute or even beautiful. After the mandatory introductions and Dionisio's apologies for the broken arm, Dionisio gave her two options where they could go, to which Melinda answered that anywhere was fine with her.

Dionisio took her for a walk around La Costa's historical sites, the cathedral with the small plaza next to it, the park serving as a reminder of the heroic battles, etc. They walked for a few hours because Dionisio thought that was the best way to know the city and Melinda liked the idea. During that time, Dionisio learned about Melinda's life. He was legitimately interested about the ethnological studies she did and asked several questions that impressed Melinda. When Melinda finished telling him about her life, Dionisio gave her a summary of his. After the walk, Dionisio invited her to have dinner at a typical and not inexpensive restaurant of the region, where they continued their chat, touching on topics of religion, politics, love, and movies. They realized they could talk about controversial topics without getting upset or frustrated even when their opinions were different. Of course, this could have been because of the respect and courtesy people usually have when they just have met. The evening progressed to the point when the waiters started looking at them with anxious stares because Dionisio and Melinda were the last costumers in the restaurant, and they needed to close for the night. They apologized, drank the last sips from the coffee cups that were refilled at least a few times, and after leaving a very generous tip, they left to find Dionisio's car. Once at his parents' house, both said their goodbyes and Dionisio asked her boldly if she would like to go out again the next weekend.

That same evening, Claudia was with Juan Carlos choosing and buying a cake for the wedding. However, neither the meringues nor the vanilla or chocolate flavors could distract her mind from the thoughts of what Dionisio and Melinda might be doing. She pictured them walking barefoot on the beach, dancing in a club, watching the sun set behind the mountains and the spectacle of colors around it, without considering that the day was overcast. At the end, Juan Carlos was the one that chose the cake because Claudia was unable to do so. In reality, at that moment, she could not care less about the cake. Her mind wandered even more that night. In bed, after a love making session that tasted flat and with no signs of the orange orchard, Claudia decided to think about Dionisio. She imagined that she was Ena or Verunje or any other of the women that had interacted with Dionisio. She was jealous; jealous of those women that had the chance but did not know how to love him. She was angered as well; angry at Melinda, and wished that Melinda would take the first flight or ship back to England.

Claudia woke up in an unnaturally bad mood and paid little attention to the breakfast Juan Carlos had lovingly prepared. She ate it to show a little courtesy, but in reality, she wanted to be as far away as possible from her fiancé. She smelled like sex, not the enjoyable one, but the one in which she was just a warm body, an object, an assistant to the solitary masturbation of her partner. She stood up to shower and remove that awful smell. Under the shower, once she felt clean and free of any particle reminding her of Juan Carlos, her mind traveled to corners that she knew existed but denied it. There she met Dionisio. For an instant, she hated him, but without a sensible reason. She cursed him at the same time a heat wave started to move around her body. It was a fulminant attack; she couldn't help but yield to those feelings. Standing up in the shower, mixing the soap and the orange scents, Claudia needed very little time to finish something she had not done in such a long time that it seemed unknown and probably forbidden. And as such, she enjoyed it enormously because she was reminded of the times that she needed no one, when there was not a man in her life to satisfy her, when Juan Carlos was not even an idea. She did not need him. But she was trapped. She felt hate filling her thoughts, sometimes directed towards Juan Carlos, sometimes directed towards Dionisio.

She exited the bathroom with the resolve to forget everything and anyone; she wanted to disappear completely from Dionisio's mind, but when she entered her bedroom wrapped in a towel, she found a naked Juan Carlos waiting for her with a magnificent erection. Claudia closed her eyes, let the towel fell to the floor to reveal her nakedness, and let herself be taken again by that man. When Juan Carlos ended, Claudia rapidly dressed and left the house without a destination.

Part 23

Café Mozart was as small coffee shop with a few tables and a concert piano in the middle, where every Tuesday a musician student would play for the costumers, giving the café an intellectual atmosphere, and making them feel that the overpriced coffee and pastries were worth it because they were listening to popular Mozart or Beethoven piano concertos. Café Mozart's popularity was incredible and it was one of the preferred places for Dionisio to grab a small bite to eat, and thought that it would be an ideal place for him to take Melinda, which could be followed by a nice walk on the beach. Dionisio surprised himself about the attention to details he was using to prepare his second date with Melinda. He was really impressed about her after their first outing, and also realized that he had a nascent itch that he wanted to scratch about this British woman.

"Hello, how are you?" asked Dionisio when he arrived to pick up Melinda at his parents' house.

"Very well. Thank you for inviting me again." answered a well-dressed and groomed Melinda that looked even more astonishing than the Melinda Dionisio had met a week ago.

"I am so happy that you two are getting along together, you make a very lovely couple." Dionisio's mother mentioned casually while coming out from the kitchen to greet her son.

Dionisio hugged his mother and kissed her on the cheek, at the same time he ignored his mother's comment.

"Well now, don't waste time here with me, go now that the evening is young."
Melinda and Dionisio looked at each other and without further ado, said goodbye to Mrs. Diosdado. Café Mozart was full to capacity, but Dionisio knew this in advance and made a reservation that shortened their wait time to only forty-five minutes. They did not care much about the wait, they were enjoying each other's company and the piano music, as well as the conversation that spurred about their favorite classical composer and then moved to the Ecuadorian tribes, the Galapagos Islands, turtles, and ending before they were seated with the life and works of Charles Darwin, which Melinda considered to be one of the persons with the most influence on human history, not only because of the impact he had in the biological sciences, but also because he was a true British.

The evening consisted of a parade of coffee cups, a couple of cake slices that both shared, and when they finished right when the sun was setting, they left for a walk on the beach. Dionisio, like a true gentleman, offered her his arm to hold, and like a romantic couple from a black and white movie, they walked along the avenue until they found the ocean, welcoming them with a lovely breeze and the constant enchanting murmur of the waves. They stayed admiring the ocean in the darkness for more than half an hour in comfortable silence.

When Dionisio left Melinda at his parents' house, they hugged with an embrace that left not a single space between the two of them.

Part 24

"Why haven't you called me?"

"I haven't had the time, I have been busy."

"You have always been busy. Are you upset with me?"

"Not at all," Claudia lied, "as I told you, I was just busy. Why didn't you call me?"

"I was busy as well…anyway, how is the wedding stuff coming along?" asked Dionisio, trying to bring the conversation to calmer waters.

There was a long pause. Through the telephone piece, Claudia's agitated breathing could be heard. The last time they had talked to each other was three weeks ago. Dionisio had indeed been extremely busy at work trying to fix a terrible sample mixing that a complete idiot had mislabeled, causing a nightmare, which could very well end in a terrible and costly legal battle. Of course, despite that someone else had made the mistake, Dionisio was the one held responsible. Despite the turmoil at work, Dionisio saw Melinda for a third time on a sunny Friday afternoon, ending with another dinner. He arranged the meeting because he missed her. However, their time together was brief because Dionisio needed all the possible time to put out the fire at work. Similarly, as in the previous occasions, Dionisio and Melinda had a great time together and ended the evening with a small and short kiss on the lips. After three weeks of intense work, Dionisio and his team were able to rectify the mistakes made.

"We are making some progress."
"You don't sound too enthusiastic, are you ok?"
"I told you already."
"I am sorry if I interrupted you."
"Do not hang up." ordered Claudia
"Why?"
"Your mind is full of Melinda, right?"
"What are you talking about?"
"I am saying that you do not need me anymore, you have taken me out of your mind and she is there in my place."
"That, besides being a stupid comment, is a lie. You will be forever with me. Always."
"I don't believe it."

Juan Carlos noted that Claudia was not the same. She had the peculiarity of being the same predictable person with her family and friends, but for some months, maybe a year, Juan Carlos realized that his fiancé was, as he liked to put it, 'on a different wavelength' that increased day after day, sometimes being completely absentminded. She would not talk with the frequency she used to; now she would remain quiet for long periods of time, even during conversations in which the words directed at her bounced back as if they had found an invisible wall. It seemed as if she was thinking or planning something. Juan Carlos guessed that it was the stress of the upcoming wedding.

He decided to let her solve her own conflicts, and he was sure that after the wedding she would come back to being the same person. At the same time, Juan Carlos tried to be with her as much as possible, he tried not to work at home or go to the office during the weekends. He spent a lot of time with her and he would call her at work at least a couple of times a day. Their telephone conversations were short but made Juan Carlos feel that he was doing the right thing.

Claudia's interest for the wedding dwindled, making Juan Carlos take the initiative to finish the last details himself. Claudia was there and pretended to be excited but it was clear to everyone that that was not the case. Juan Carlos, however, never asked her if she wanted to postpone or cancel the wedding. He thought it was a natural stage for his soon to be wife. He was mistaken.

Part 25

La Principal was named as such when the first inhabitants of the regions arrived to La Costa from the internal regions of the country. They opened a small pathway at the bottom of the mountain range to help transport construction material to the future city of La Costa. At the beginning, this pathway was just a clearing surrounded by bush where chariots pulled by horses and mules precariously moved. The pathway followed a parallel direction between the mountain range and the seashore. As people started to populate the region, more and more bush was cleared to build houses and businesses, and new pathways branched away from the main pathways or La Principal. In an orderly fashion, the people named each ramification La Primera, La Segunda, La

Tercera, and so on. From La Principal, between La Séptima and La novena, a pathway branched off leading to the sea, and was called La Costa. As La Costa grew, La Principal grew in length and width, turning from a simple pathway into a dusty road, then to a very broad paved street bordered with business and houses owned by the important people of the region. Eventually, La Principal developed into a three-lane road with each direction divided by a narrow median. La Principal also had a lateral road for each direction separated between the interior lanes by a wide sidewalk. These sidewalks were full of small flower beds, sculptures, gazebos, fountains, magazine stands, benches and tables. La Principal turned into a place where people would spend the weekends walking; entertained by musicians, jugglers, mimes, poets, painters, and many others that would establish themselves along the 5 kilometer stretch of La Principal.

Melinda fell in love with this avenue from the first time she walked there, and when she had the time she would walk along its length. She liked to sit down on the benches and look at people's faces that walked in front of her. As a good ethnologist, she looked at them trying to extract their stories, experiences, and what they had lived through. Sometimes she would make up long tales about their lives, mixing with them beings from other times and cultures, gods, and unknown heroes. She enjoyed this activity so much that sometimes she would laugh out loud causing the people around her to think that the young lady on the bench was borderline crazy.

One Sunday afternoon, as she watched a fat mime performing a less than original routine of being inside an invisible cube that few people cared to watch. Armando, El Negro, sat beside her. Melinda did not pay much attention to him because it was normal for strangers to share benches. But El Negro stared at her every now and then, causing Melinda to ask sharply what he was looking at. El Negro, who was not shy and very bold, replied that it was rare to see such a beautiful woman watching a mime. Melinda did not react to what he said because it sounded insincere, but she could not stop looking at the medium built man, with firm muscles, a bit ugly but interesting, and with a very dark brown skin that almost appeared to be dark green. El Negro introduced himself as Armando Legorrea, but immediately mentioned to her that everybody called him El Negro. Melinda introduced herself, but since she had her doubts about that man called El Negro, she introduced herself as Claudia. *Does Claudia have a last name?* asked El Negro, to what Melinda answered immediately, *Just Claudia to you.* They chatted some, but in reality, it was almost a monologue about El Negro's life that Melinda listened to while watching the fat mime that now pretended to be going up an escalator. El Negro mentioned that he was born and raised in La Costa and that he was a direct descendent of one of the original families that founded the city. He also mentioned about the many skills he had, or at least he thought he had. At the end of his monologue, when Melinda just responded by nodding, El Negro gave her a business card and pointed to the telephone number where she could reach him if she wanted to have a good time. Melinda took it with the thought to trash it as soon as she could find a garbage can. El Negro, just as the way he appeared, left her there on the bench.

El Negro indeed came from one of the first families that settled in La Costa, and thanks to this historical chance and the financial vision of one of his great-great-great-great relatives, the Legorrea family accumulated a considerable amount of wealth. El Negro had everything he needed and much more, and had no necessity of getting a job because his future and the future of his children's children's children was completely secure. Despite his family's wealth, El Negro studied law in a very prestigious university in Europe. When he finished his studies, he returned to La Costa because, according to him, there was no other place on the planet better to live. He established a small law buffet which boomed into one of the most important firms in the country.

Several days passed before Melinda found El Negro's business card in a little wicker basket on top of Dionisio's nightstand. She looked at the card not very sure of what to do with it; she thought for a second and decided to tear it up into little pieces, but right as she was about to do it, she grabbed the phone in Dionisio's room and called the number on the card. El Negro answered as if he were in a rush, making Melinda hesitate. Thankfully Melinda remembered that she had introduced herself as Claudia and said that name when she introduced herself again over the phone, reminding him of how they had met.

"Ah, right!" said El Negro, followed immediately by a litany of activities he had in front of him for the day. Melinda could not care less about all that and was very close to hanging up. Suddenly, El Negro asked her if she wanted to go out with him to a meeting he had planned for the weekend with a business partner. Somehow, Melinda said yes and gave him the address of the Diosdado's home, but was not very sure what she had signed up for with this man.

Friday arrived, and El Negro came to pick her up. When he rang the bell, Dionisio's father opened the door and was surprised to realize that El Negro asked for Claudia.

"Claudia?" asked Dionisio's dad, and when El Negro was going to say something, Melinda appeared coming down the stairs.

"He is coming to pick me up," said Melinda to Mr. Diosdado, while he stood there confused. There was a quick introduction that left Mr. Diosdado with his mouth open when he found out that the person in front of him was from the Legorrea family. As quickly as El Negro had arrived, he left with Melinda because he was late for his meeting. When Mrs. Diosdado was told that El Negro Legorrea had picked Melinda up, she was almost happily surprised but turned rapidly upset knowing that Melinda was not being honest with her son by going out with another man.

In the car, El Negro told Melinda where they were going to go, what the specialty of the restaurant was, and a little history about his business partner. They arrived to La Onceava where they found the restaurant named 32, a very pretentious place with long windows instead of walls, tables with little lamps, and voluptuous waitresses with very short skirts. El Negro parked in the valet area, got out of the car, and like a true gentleman, opened Melinda's door and helped her out. The restaurant's staff recognized El Negro immediately and quickly guided him directly to a corner table where his partner and his fiancée were already waiting for him, both enjoying a white anis-flavored spirit. The evening ended up being very interesting and amusing, and Melinda enjoyed El Negro's company. Once the night was upon them, El Negro stood up to say that he and Claudia needed to leave. Melinda did not understand why they had to leave when she was having such a great time, and had no choice but to say her goodbyes and leave with El Negro. El Negro talked while driving to Dionisio's parents but she would not remember that conversation because she had had a little too much to drink. As a gentleman, again, El Negro walked Melinda to the house door. They hugged their goodbyes. That night, Melinda slept deeply.

The next day, Melinda recalled how nice the evening was with El Negro and the other two, and concluded that he was a really nice person, entertaining, and he had respected her. She liked him. She grabbed the phone and called Dionisio's apartment. He answered, not too happy, but was glad that Melinda was on the other side. Melinda lost no time to tell Dionisio that she had a great time last night with El Negro.

"What Negro?" replied Dionisio, followed by Melinda saying 'Legorrea'.

"El Negro Legorrea?" asked Dionisio, not knowing where this conversation was leading. Melinda then told him about how they had met and about their evening together. At the end, Melinda told him that she thought that she was in love with El Negro. This news was like a bucket of frigid water being poured over Dionisio's head. *You are such a whore, Melinda*, said Dionisio to himself.

Part 26

His hands were sweaty and his stomach was in nauseating knots, making him feel that vomiting was a welcome option. Despite these tricks that his body was playing on him, he decided to continue with his plan to call Melinda and tell her that she was beautiful and that he would like to have a semi-serious relationship with her beyond friendship, whatever that meant. The only thing that he remembered that afternoon while he was driving was that he was practicing his love monologue.

"Why haven't you called me?" said Claudia, with an upset tone in her voice but at the same time relieved that Dionisio had contacted her.

"I was sick of my heart," he answered, as if he were talking to his mother.

Dionisio explained to her that he had one of his episodes that left him in bed for a while; an episode that was strong and set in his mind the idea that he was going to die soon, an episode that maybe was the worst he had ever had.

The Death was bored, sitting at the curb of the sidewalk like a nice little girl, watching the cars move along La Novena while counting the days every driver had left on this planet. One of them, The Death realized, was Dionisio, and just for spite and to entertain herself, she squeezed Dionisio's heart. But she was careless and squeezed it more than what she was planning to do, sending Dionisio to the emergency room. He did not want to go to the hospital, but because he had the episode while he was driving, he had to stop in the middle of La Novena to avoid crashing. He was somewhat lucky that a police car was not too far behind him, and when the furious police officer walked to his car in the middle of the street, he quickly realized that something was very wrong with the purple-faced driver. Dionisio was taken to the closest hospital in an ambulance where they examined his heart and he was more or less stabilized. He spent a few nights in the hospital in solitude, because the doctors could not find an emergency contact for him, and when he regained consciousness he did not call anyone to avoid worrying his parents. After talking to his cardiologist that prescribed novel medications that may help him, he was released.

Claudia was greatly mortified when she heard the entirety of the story, she told him not to move from his office because she was going to go there immediately. She did so, and when she arrived, she hugged him for a long time and gave him a nice kiss on his neck. Dionisio felt as if he were in a very secure place in her arms, like being protected by his mother's arms when he was a kid. Claudia looked at Dionisio with love and tenderness but had no words to tell him. There was a pleasant silence in which both of them recognized each other.

"You know that I am going to die young, right?"

"Don't say stupid things."

"I don't have many friends."

"So?"

"I am going to die alone, nobody is going to come to my funeral."

"Why are you so tragic?"

"Don't make fun of me, this is serious. The Death is close."

"There you go again saying stupid things," answered Claudia with tears in her eyes.

"It is useless to talk to you about these things, Claudia!"

"I am sorry, ok, continue."

"I know very few people; I don't have friends, and nobody will come to my funeral."

"Your parents and family will surely be there."

"Of course, but…"

"And I will be there."

"Is that a promise?"

"Dionisio," Claudia's eyes were now overflowing with love and compassion; she took his hand and continued, "I promise you that the day you die, wherever you are, I will be there with you."

Dionisio smiled little.

Part 27

Dionisio dialed his parents' telephone number to say hello and also to see how Melinda was doing. His father answered and immediately chastised him about not communicating with them, to which Dionisio answered that he had a lot of work and that they were welcome to call him anytime they wanted if they were worried about him. There was a pause in which Dionisio realized how he had spoken with little respect to his father. He apologized, and Mr. Diosdado redirected the conversation as a sign that he was not offended. After talking for a while, Dionisio told his father that he had spent a few days in the hospital. The reply was immediate, and both Mr. and Mrs. Diosdado (who was already listening to the conversation in the other telephone set) scolded, chastised and exhorted him as if he were a seven-year-old kid. Dionisio had no option but to apologize and confirm many times that he was feeling well and that he was taking a new medication that appeared to be working, and that if there were another episode he would immediately communicate with them. Also, he asked them to put Melinda on the phone. She was still sleeping, but Mrs. Diosdado woke her up. After Dionisio's complaints to his mom because there was no need to wake her up, Melinda answered and talked for a while. Melinda told him that she had gone out with El Negro a couple more times and that she was starting to have stronger feelings for him. El

Negro offered her a job as his personal assistant and would be happy to find for her a nice place to live by herself, clarifying that she liked living with Dionisio's parents' house but, as she told herself when she left England, she wanted to be free and not being a burden to anyone.

"Did you hear me Dionisio?" she asked when there was no indication of his voice on the other side. He replied saying that that was a great idea and he was happy that she had found someone like El Negro Legorrea. At the end of their conversation, Dionisio, as a last resort, asked her if she wanted to go out for a coffee at the end of the day. Melinda had to decline the offer because she had already made plans with her new boyfriend.

The desert extended to the horizon to fuse with a sky covered by a homogeneous layer of infinite clouds. Right in the middle of the desert there was the skull and horns of a buffalo, and beside them, Dionisio was sitting on a white sheet. The night fell and a small oil lamp close to Dionisio started to emit light. As the darkness increased, the brightness of the oil lamp became more intense. Millions of insects of all kinds and shape started to fly, crawl, and migrate towards the light. Dionisio was incapable of doing anything, the attack was very effective and deadly: the insects crawled into any exposed hole in Dionisio's body and methodically ate Dionisio from the inside out. At the end, Dionisio's skeleton remained in the same position as he was when alive. When the oil lamp extinguished its light, the bones of what was once Dionisio collapsed and turned into dust. Dionisio woke up drenched in a cold sweat and with very weak and shaky arms. In front of him was The Death, that looked at him with the same eyes that Claudia had when he lost himself in them while reflecting the sea from the bridge. *I will take care of everything, as I have always done,* was what Dionisio understood The Death told him. Dionisio woke up for a second time and found himself in his bedroom, completely terrified.

Part 28

Juan Carlos' aunt, a heavy lady with a round Russian-doll looking face, was walking absentmindedly in one of Monserrat's park, enjoying the breeze and the sunny blue sky. As it was her custom, she left the stoned path at the usual spot to walk barefoot and feel the softness of the grass blades. She walked through a not very popular area just minding her solitude and the quietness around her, until her body fell into a hidden hole in the ground. Maybe it was a hole someone dug or maybe it was a small sinkhole, but that was not really relevant because the important part was that the hole was smaller than the circumference of her waist, causing the aunt to become trapped with half of her body over the surface and half under it. When she was found, two days later, drenched by the rain, she appeared to be sleeping with her arms stretched out and her face tilted towards her right shoulder. Her eyes were closed and her face was peaceful. They took her out of the hole by digging around her, and grabbing her at the same time to avoid her falling further into the dark mouth below. She was taken to the emergency room, but it was obvious that there was nothing else that could have been done. The doctors concluded that she died of exhaustion, probably while trying to free herself from the hole that wanted to eat her alive. Juan Carlos' parents called him to let him know about his aunt passing, and without hesitation, he decided to travel to Monserrat to the funeral. Claudia wanted to go with him but Juan Carlos insisted that it was not necessary; he appreciated the offer, but preferred for her to stay. She agreed, without causing any discussion, and probably it was for the better. On top of that, she had never met the aunt before she had died in the hole.

Claudia felt free the Saturday morning that she woke up without Juan Carlos beside her. She got up, prepared a coffee and a simple breakfast of bread with butter and strawberry jam, and as if were pre-established, she thought about Dionisio. That Saturday, Claudia called Dionisio to talk to him. They greeted each other, trying to find the right words, and then Claudia told him in detail about the aunt's death. Dionisio's reaction was first to say I am sorry, but then he burst into laughter, immediately apologizing and justifying himself by saying that the story was somewhat funny. Claudia did not find it funny and reproached him. After many 'I'm sorry', Dionisio ended that part of the conversation by commenting that someone had probably dug the hole. Claudia ignored the comment.

Both felt as if they were talking to a stranger, but at the same time, they felt that they were very intimate, as if they had just woken up side by side. They chatted for a long time and Claudia, without thinking twice, invited him for dinner at her place.

"Are you sure?" asked a concerned Dionisio, to what Claudia answered that she was completely sure about it. Dionisio arrived that afternoon holding a flower bouquet, a gesture with the intention of being thankful, and only that. Claudia accepted the flowers happily, jumping on her feet and clapping like a little girl; a bit ridiculous for her age. She cooked spaghetti a la carbonara that ended up being really tasty. The

meal was accompanied by an imported white wine.
They talked about many things for a few hours, and
when the evening was turning into night and the wine
was running out, Dionisio thanked her and poised
himself to leave. Claudia asked him to stay a little
longer because she had a surprise for him. Dionisio
agreed. She disappeared to her bedroom while
Dionisio waited, browsing some magazines covering
a little table in the living room. The surprise was when
he lifted his eyes, finding Claudia almost in complete
nakedness covering the entrance to the living room.
She was only wearing dark blue panties with some
wavy ornaments that left the lower part of the butt
free, and from there, her glorious legs descended like
magnificent pillars, those legs that Dionisio adored.
He felt a knot in his stomach. Claudia called him and
he obeyed, as if enchanted. He moved very close to
her and with his hands he pushed her closer to him;
he passed his hands softly over much of her body,
guiding himself by her curvy silhouette, enjoying her
round butt cheeks that he had dreamed of caressing
thoroughly many times, while Claudia emitted soft
moans as she departed to the orange orchards.
Dionisio smelled the orange scent coming out of the
skin of that woman, and also felt his heart beating at
the same rhythm as hers, as if they were only one. He
held her tight against his body to feel as much of her
as possible. For a moment, they fused with each
other into a mass that left no space between the two
of them, and only because of her nakedness and
Dionisio fully clothed, it was possible to distinguish
who was who. A mirror that was inside Claudia's
bedroom facing them replicated with high fidelity their
reality, and it called Dionisio's attention. He looked at
it and saw himself hugging a naked Dionisio; or was
Claudia hugging herself? The vision startled him and

immediately he felt his heart beat abnormally. She pushed her away with some force, telling her that they could not continue.

"Why not?" was her reply.

"Because all this will end; you are mine, but you do not belong to me."

"Is it Melinda?" asked Claudia, with tears in her eyes and disapproval on her face.

"It's a lot of things," he said.

"But I'm fine as I am; are you believing what Verunje told you? Do you think you will be happy like that? The only thing you are doing is fooling yourself. Melinda doesn't want you because El Negro took her away from you!"

"I'm leaving," said Dionisio, upset.

"Go if you wish! But I am going to tell you just one thing: when you cross that door, there is no coming back!"

He opened the door, then turned around to see a crouching Claudia, covered in tears and yelling at him to forget about her forever.

That night, Claudia's mind traveled long distances through deserted lands that expanded in all four directions. She was alone. She thought that she was running or maybe flying. She could see the sand below her, but could not feel it. The sky was blue without a single cloud and the sun was intensely projecting Claudia's shadow onto the sand. She traveled long distances running or flying, she couldn't tell, until she saw in the distance a still ocean that appeared blue and green when she was over it. She finally realized that she was flying, and found herself reflected on the mirror formed by still waters. Her image was perfect: she could see every detail of her naked body and it made her feel goosebumps. It was not her body; she closed her eyes and when she opened them again, Dionisio was staring at her intensely.

That same night, Melinda dreamed with a large valley where the snow fell rapidly. She was in the middle of it and the snow had already covered her ankles. She looked around her, but the only thing she could see was her reflection in the snow; she was tired and contemplative, maybe sleepy. The snow now covered all her legs up to her waist, but she was not cold, she was very comfortable as if she were in her own bed. When she looked again, the snow had disappeared and she found herself on a small bed with white sheets and cushioned walls. She felt at home, in Oxford. She looked again and the small bed had turned into a coffin: her own. She started sweating a cold sweat. She woke up. Dionisio's room was mostly dark and the first thing she saw was the curtain flapping with the wind entering the room. She heard several *clicks* that she followed with her eyes to find a white lizard looking at her close to the window. She remained awake for the rest of the night.

Part 29

Las Granadas Park was off La Tercera, a short walk away from Mr. and Mrs. Diosdado's house. It was a nice place to promenade in the mornings or evenings because one could watch the sunrise or the sunset from its highest point in the middle of the park. When Melinda could not go to La Principal, she would happily go to Las Granadas. That cloudy November afternoon was one of those days La Principal was too far away. She'd had a terrible night and felt like something the cat dragged in, and thought that a little exercise would be good for her mood. The park was unusually empty and the breeze lifting some of the dried leaves gave it a creepy atmosphere. Also, from the moment she arrived to the park, she felt as if someone were watching her from the distance. Thus, she looked over her shoulder constantly to see if someone was following her. Only once could she see a silhouette that she thought was a woman's figure scurrying through the bushes. She thought she was hallucinating. She decided to go back home, leave the walking for another occasion, and call El Negro to see how he was doing. While climbing the street that would take her to the house, Melinda felt the ground move and a sensation of fading away inundated her from the feet to the head. She leaned on the wall of a house but the wall could not catch her as she collapsed to the ground, losing all consciousness. Dionisio, that had told his parents he was going to go that day to their house saw an inert body spread on the sidewalk. He stopped the car and quickly got out to help. He quickly noticed it was Melinda, especially when he saw her cast. He held her in his arms looking at her face that was paler than usual. Without hesitation, Dionisio carried Melinda to the car and took her to his parents' house.

Mr. Diosdado and Dionisio took Melinda to her room. They removed her tennis shoes and without undressing her they put her under the bed sheets. Dionisio advised his parents not to call the doctor or take her to emergencies, the best thing was for Melinda to rest. He mentioned that probably her blood pressure was a little low.

That night Melinda dreamed about the same snowy valley where a massive buffalo roamed gingerly. On top of the buffalo was Dionisio and a strange woman, they were fused by their backs as if there were Siamese twins, but in reality, they look like a big barrel with two heads. Melinda woke up abruptly in the middle of the night, turned the light on to find the same lizard she saw on the wall in a previous occasion. She quickly got out of bed to search for her bags, clothes and other belongings, and quietly to avoid waking up the Diosdado's, left into the night of La Costa that looked darker than ever.

The moon was red and full, but lacked brightness; an omen of sorts to the people of La Costa. That night a bus full of passengers going to the capital city skidded at the edge of La Costa city limits while climbing the mountain ridge, falling into an abyss where darkness and La Muerte devoured each and every one of the passengers. That same night, a small ship carrying several members of the coast guard sank after colliding with another ship that was invisible to the first one because it had no lights or flags that could warn anyone of its presence. This tragedy became absurd when all the coast guard members on the boat but one drown, but all the passengers of the second ship survived. Three car accidents happened as well during that night, all in close proximity to each other. The first one was because of a drunk driver crashing into a utility pole; the air bags inflated, saving him from imminent death, however, the pole splintered in three large pieces, one of them flying as a projectile towards a window of a house where a woman was resting peacefully in her bed. The enormous piece of pole crashed mercilessly against her skull killing her immediately. In the second accident, two cars rammed in a head-on collision with each other; both drivers had neglected the use of seatbelts and were expelled through the windshields, landing against the remains of the opposite car's windshield. Both died instantly. The third accident happened when an ambulance that carried the only coast guard survivor from the shipwrecks encountered oil leaking from the car that had smashed against the utility pole a few minutes before. The ambulance lost control, flipped, and skidded for several meters. The only person that died was the coast guard. While all these tragedies happened and the rest of La Costa slept, Melinda snuck out the Diosdados' home with all of her belongings hanging from her back. She did not know where to go, she only knew she needed to get out of there as fast as possible.

Part 30

Early in the morning Dionisio's parents called him to let him know that Melinda had disappeared and that the police were already looking for her. They never heard anything about her again. Many years later, in the cold waters of the British Islands seas, the remnants of a skeleton washed up to shore. It was only a skull and a few cervical vertebrae dragging a colorless and salty shirt. Nobody knew who that person was but the inhabitants of the region buried the bones as if they had belonged to a close relative.

Dionisio

Part 1

The telephone rang several times until a woman with hands covered by dark spots indicating rapid aging picked it up. Her voice was like a sweet grandmother that had lived a life full of happiness.

"Hello?"

"Hello mother."

"My son! Blessed are the ears that hear your voice, how are you?"

"Very well mother, you?"

"As always, with pain in my hands and knees, but overall, I cannot complain."

"I see…and father?"

"Obsessed with his collection of miniature airplanes. You know him, since he retired that is the only thing he does. But you, tell me, how are you? Everything ok?"

"As I said mother, very well, I just wanted to say hello."

"When are you coming to visit us? You have not been here in a long time and we don't live too far away from you. I think I see more often your cousin Pili that lives in Alta Vista, and that is much farther away."

There was a pause while Dionisio searched for the right words to say.

"I am going to live in Salamanca," Dionisio threw the words at her as if they were burning his tongue.

"What? Why? Remember the reason we left everything in Salamanca was to live in La Costa because of your heart. You can't go there." she answered, as if she were talking to a seven-year-old child.

"I am already in Salamanca, mother."

Mrs. Diosdado could not answer because she did not know what to say.

"Thank you, mother, for worrying about me, and thank you for the sacrifice you and dad made for my health, but I had to go; I had to get out of La Costa, I could not stand my life there."

"But…you could…die;" she said this last word very softly, "your heart…"

"My heart," Dionisio interrupted, "put a chain around my neck and tied me to La Costa. I need to free myself from it, from my heart." Dionisio did not believe his own words.

"I don't understand!" said his mother almost crying.

"Mother, this is better for everyone. I just wanted to let you know that I am in Salamanca, all my business in La Costa are finalized, you do not have to do a thing for me there."

"Oh, my son!" she exclaimed.

"Don't worry mother, I will be fine. I will call you sometime later to say hello to father and give you my new address."

"Ok." sounded a very sad voice on the other side.

"I love you mother."

But Mrs. Diosdado had already hung up the phone and could not hear this last part. Dionisio was sitting at the edge of his bed and did not bother to hang up the phone on its base; a long monotonous tone filled the room.

The first hours of that night were darker than usual. Outside, a strong March storm punished the city and the uninterrupted howl of the wind quenched the outside noise. Dionisio thought that going to sleep would be a good idea. His dream was intense, there were no buffalos or snow, this time it was the immensity of the ocean, expanding itself invisible in the darkness of the night. He knew it was the ocean, the sound and the breeze that hit his face while we flew above it were unmistakable. He flew in circles, large ones, and did not know why but he knew that if he stopped he would lose himself in the deep of the ocean. And he flew, and flew, and flew, and as he did, his body tensed up and he felt that his strength was abandoning him. When he gave in, the waters called to him with an intense magnetism, and as he plummeted to his end, he woke up. He was sweating and his heart beat had no rhythm. He lacked air. He quickly stood up, causing his vision to go grey, he sat down to recover and let the grayness pass. He then moved to the window, stuck his head outside, and felt the cold air that somehow soothed him. He took several deep breaths to fill his lungs with air but that was not enough to fill them. He came back inside, looked at his night stand where a collection of small prescription bottles was lined up in a row. He went close to the bottles, examined the labels and the third one was the one he was looking for. He started opening it, but then hesitated, stopped, and took another deep breath. He reached a conclusion. With bottle in hand, he went back to the window that was still open, the drapes flapping in the wind. He opened the little bottle and with one swift movement, emptied its contents onto the street below. The wind stopped for a second and he could hear the clack-clack-clack of the pills hitting the sidewalk. He ran to the nightstand, grabbed all the other little bottles and went back to the window. Precariously, he opened the little bottles and emptied all of them onto the street below.

Clack-clack-clack. He threw himself on the bed barely breathing and listened to his heart beating now fast and regular. He closed his eyes to wait for The Death, but she never arrived.

He woke up a few hours later. He was not sweating and was breathing normally, and his heart had a beautiful rhythm, as if nothing had happened. He stood up and went to the restroom to pee and take a shower. He washed himself slowly and enjoyed shaving his face. He came out of the bathroom and observed his bed, the desk, the chair, the nightstand, the couch, the unhung phone that he immediately hung up as if he were waiting for someone to call, the few bags filled with stuff, the small kitchen and the refrigerator. His life was reduced to that. He dressed, prepared a green tea that he sipped at the desk. On it, there were a few blank sheets of paper, one pen, and a few envelopes. He took the pen and tried to write something but nothing came. He proceeded with parsimony to drink his tea while he looked out the window, at the gray Salamanca on the other side.

The day passed with nothing to do. He did not want to get out into the city that saw him being born. He took a book from a bag, a thick red-covered one with the numbers two-six-six-six on its cover. He threw himself on bed and read it for a few hours. In reality, sometimes he read it and sometimes he would only look at the words on the pages without understanding their meaning while his mind traveled and got lost in other places. He battled not to reach those places, he did not want to remember all the pain he felt and the pain he had caused. He would close his eyes to concentrate on what he had done: he left La Costa to change his life; or was it to die? He would fight these thoughts in his mind and would end up exhausted. He decided to sleep; it was still clear outside, gray but clear, probably it was close to 5:00 pm. Dionisio slept the rest of the afternoon, all evening, and all night. He did not dream.

The sun woke him up. He stood up feeling much better, and looked outside the window. The new day seemed rejuvenated after all the gray days. He went to the bathroom to pee and shower, although he thought it was a useless shower because he did not feel dirty. He came out and felt very hungry for the first time in several days. He searched for a pack of peanuts in his bags but could not find it. He cursed. He dressed with some urgency and thought about going out to eat something.

Salamanca presented itself beautiful after the storms; the streets were shining and the people seemed joyful, radiant, new. For an instant, he wished he could be one of them. He entered a store, bought a sandwich and a hot coffee and got out to find a place to sit, probably in a close by park. He sat on a bench next to several sets of tables and chairs where men of different ages congregated. He looked carefully to find out they were playing backgammon. He did not know much about the game, he knew the name but had never played it. He stood up from the bench and moved closer to one of the pairs playing. He was entertained and focused, trying to understand how the game was played without interrupting the players. He then felt a tap on his right shoulder. He turned around to find a young man, maybe twenty-six or twenty-eight, of deep dark skin making the white of his eyes to come out. He was bald.

"Do you want to play?" asked the man in a friendly manner.

"Excuse me?" asked Dionisio because he did not understand the question.

"Do you want to play?" repeated the man.

"Ah…no thanks, I don't know how."

"Don't worry, I'll teach you."

Dionisio thought for a second while sipping his coffee. He did not register what was happening, he thought the man was going to rob him or ask him for money, and this thought was portrayed on his eyes.

"I'm sorry, let me introduce myself, my name is Mark, Mark Schneider." he said as he stretched his hand to shake Dionisio's.

Dionisio fumbled with his sandwich and coffee to hold them with one hand and stretched his hand to shake Mark's.

"Dionisio Diosdado." he did not feel too comfortable telling that man his real name.

"C'mon, I'll teach you."

Mark Schneider walked away to an empty table with chairs. Dionisio followed him, not very sure of himself.

Mark Schneider was a black man from Germany. He arrived to the new continent more than five years ago leaving behind his German heritage, if he had any. His parents were refugees from central Africa, one of those countries that changed names several times after each new revolution, promising prosperity and democracy. He came with them when he was a young baby. In Europe, his parents worked hard to establish a small store selling fruit, vegetables, and other foods, that thanks to Mark's father's administrative skills, turned into a small empire of stores all across Germany. The Schneiders, which in reality this last name was chosen by his father to move his family closer to the German culture, gave Mark anything he needed, and once the stores were a success and they became very wealthy, they provided to their son more that he really needed.

When Mark turned 20, he left Germany to travel the world and somehow ended up in Salamanca where he did everything and nothing, following his philosophy of enjoying every moment to the fullest, which was easy to do for someone that need not worry about money.

Dionisio played that first day several games with Mark. At the beginning, backgammon was difficult for Dionisio and a bit boring, but the more he played it, the more he would discover strategies and tricks, making the game more entertaining. During the games, Mark monopolized the conversation and talked to Dionisio about his life, to what Dionisio did not know what to do but to affirm with his head or express a few single syllable words or sounds. However, Mark's conversation was very interesting and helped Dionisio to come to a very positive conclusion about him. When allowed, after Mark had finished with his monologue, Dionisio quickly told him a few details of his life, nothing really elaborated because, although Mark seemed like a nice person, Dionisio still was not very comfortable with him.

They agreed to meet the next morning to play a new round of games. Dionisio walked back to his apartment in an improved mood and with a bag full of groceries he had bought on his way back. That afternoon and evening he stayed in the apartment reading his red book for several hours. Once ready to sleep, his mind wandered to places he would rather not visit. He stood up from bed and sat on the chair close to the desk, took a pen to write something that resulted in being meaningless. He made a ball out of the piece of paper and put it in the trash can. He started again, the first word that he wrote was Claudia, then some phrases came out of his pen but again, the result was meaningless and the piece of paper ended up in the trash. After many attempts, the trash can was almost full of paper balls. Dionisio quit his attempt to write and threw himself on the bed one more time. Finally, he was able to fall asleep. Claudia appeared in his dream, not like her but like a masculine version that looked a lot like him. Claudia approached him while the moonlight shone on their faces, and when she was a few centimeters away, he realized that it was indeed Claudia. They did not talk, they just looked at each other for a long time. At the end, Claudia turned around and left; snow started to fall.

Dionisio woke up early, had breakfast, took a shower and left towards the park to meet Mark. Mark was already playing with someone else, but when he saw Dionisio he asked him not to go away, that he would be with him soon. Dionisio stepped a few meters away and started walking in circles. Ten minutes later, Mark called to him and greeted him. They sat down and started playing a silent game interrupted infrequently by Mark to advise Dionisio on possible strategies. When they finished the first game, Mark asked Dionisio what was he doing in Salamanca. Dionisio hesitated to answer the question, but at the end he mentioned that he needed some space and freedom from his previous life.

Previous life? asked Mark. Dionisio thought about his answer and only responded that he was fed up with his life in La Costa and that he needed a change. Mark did not ask more questions but signaled him to play another game.

Dionisio and Mark saw each other on more occasions, most of the time they were in the park playing backgammon and sometimes Mark would invite him to his apartment to watch a movie or for dinner. It was obvious to Dionisio that Mark liked the good life: he lived in an apartment that occupied an entire floor of what was not a small building. Most of the walls in the apartment did not reach the ceiling and it made the apartment to resemble a labyrinth. There was a living room with black furniture and a lot of little lamps coming out of the ceiling hanging from a flexible wire, like inverted tulips. The kitchen was massively spacious and was equipped with the best appliances, as far as Dionisio could tell. There was only on bedroom connected to the living room by a zigzagging hallway, which forked in the middle to reach the bathroom and the toilet, the only room in the entire apartment where the walls reached the ceiling. One door after the bathroom there was another door opening to the closet, which occupied an immense amount of space that looked more like a warehouse than a closet.

Dionisio learned that Mark was an excellent cook with an ample repertoire of dishes that never repeated.

Their friendship grew and turned more intimate. On one occasion, while dining in Mark's apartment, Mark told Dionisio that he was not attracted to women, something that worried Dionisio at the moment, but he was relieved when Mark mentioned that he was not attracted to men either.

"Then what the heck do you like?" asked Dionisio.

"Nothing;" said Mark, "neither women nor men, I am asexual and I could care less about sex." Dionisio did not know what to do with that information. Then Mark asked him, "And you? What do you like, women or sheep?"

"That's not really funny," said Dionisio, "but I like women of course."

"And who is the lucky one that freed herself from you?"

Dionisio had been able to distract himself from Claudia thanks to his friendship with Mark; he'd been sleeping well and had very few dreams, and his heart was behaving properly. He did not try again to write that letter or whatever it was that was in his mind from the day he left La Costa. For some weeks, he almost forgot about Claudia. *Forget Claudia? Was that even possible?* He tried it many times and many times he failed. He would remember Claudia on that day, her eyes full of tears, yelling at him to forget about her. He knew that Claudia had deep roots inside his mind and heart and that only The Death would be able, maybe, to remove her from him. That is why Dionisio's face darkened when Mark asked that question.

He almost left Mark's apartment at that very moment, but he felt that Mark was a safe place for him and maybe he would be helpful to rid him of her. Dionisio opened his mouth and with a very detailed explanation, told Mark more than he ever wanted to know. When the evening ended, Dionisio left to his apartment and cried long hours until he fell asleep. When the sun rose again, Dionisio woke up feeling well. He thought that good fortune had planted Mark in his path and for the first time in a long time, he felt free from that woman. That Sunday morning in Salamanca, for the first time in many months, Dionisio felt alive.

Part 2

From the bridge, he watched the seagulls flying in circles above the deep blue sea. He was hoping, against his will, to see her one more time to tell her all the many things he had in his mind, but she never came. He finished his ham sandwich, cleaned his mouth with a paper napkin, and with no remorse, turned around to march to his office. He took a cardboard box full of books, journals, and other items. He went to the door, looked around to make sure he had everything with him, and left his office for the last time. He walked slowly along an empty hallway towards the elevators without looking behind. He arrived to his car, placing his box on the passenger's seat. He started driving towards De La Costa, then north to reach La Principal, he crossed La Tercera, and when he was close by, he looked nostalgically in the direction of his parents' house for a moment. As he continued driving, the road disappeared between the cloud covered mountains, suggesting rain and fog for the first few hours of driving.

It did not take him much time to decide to get out of La Costa. After Melinda's disappearance, Dionisio could not stop thinking that in some way or another he was directly or indirectly involved in it. Was he? His recurrent dreams during the time Melinda left would take him to a large cliff several kilometers away north of La Costa, where the ocean's waves would break aggressively against the sharpened rocks that look like hungry teeth at the bottom of it. He could see, there, Melinda's face full of horror and fear while falling at an extraordinarily slow speed. Dionisio would see The Death with Claudia's eyes laughing hard out loud about that tragic scene she was witnessing, *or was she part of it?* When Melinda would reach the bottom of the cliff and her body would bend and splatter like a broken egg, The Death's voice would whisper in Dionisio's ear that he could be happy again. Invariably, Dionisio would wake up in a fog and shaky for the rest of the day.

During the first few days, the police did nothing about Melinda's disappearance, telling Mr. and Mrs. Diosdado to wait a few days and to try to reach Melinda's relatives in Oxford, because there was a very reasonable chance that the young lady simply decided to go home. Dionisio's parents had no idea how to get in contact with the Ramsden family, and even through El Negro Legorrea's efforts, who maintained almost a daily contact with the Diosdados in case they heard something about Melinda, and the top-notch private detectives he hired that searched frantically and called many numbers and travelled to many cities, not a single clue about Melinda's whereabouts was found. It was as if Melinda had never existed, as if she were only a collective mirage, one of life's cruel practical jokes.

After a week, the La Costa police, maybe due to the constant chastising coming from El Negro, decided to look at Melinda's disappearance. They interviewed and questioned every single person that could have met Melinda, not many since she did not have that many friends in La Costa, and reached the conclusion that the only one that could have been involved in Melinda's fate was Dionisio. However, this was just speculation, since the police had not a single piece of evidence to prove this theory.

Silence flooded the lives of the Dionisio, Mr. and Mrs. Diosdado who were also living in a void that depressed their mood constantly. They tried, individually, to entertain themselves and forget the many days where their lives stood to a stop trying to find the smallest clue about Melinda. Sometimes, not often, Dionisio's parents would call him to let him know what he already knew: there were zero clues about her, but the real reason of those calls was to make sure Dionisio was doing ok. Eventually, the calls stopped.

The nightly news on the television, thanks to El Negro's popularity, took advantage of Melinda's disappearance, squeezing out any conspiracy theory that would increase their ratings: she was in England with her forgotten children; she was in South America as a member of one of the tribes she studied; she was still in La Costa under a pseudonym and with a new face thanks to plastic surgery.

December and its holidays arrived without making any noise. The Diosdados prepared a simple dinner and added an extra plate to the table to remember Melinda or maybe in case she showed up with a big smile on her face. Dionisio arrived to his parents' house as he would always do for Christmas Eve. He ate, talked to his parents, and left. When he arrived home, the thought came to his mind: Claudia's wedding had already happened and he had forgotten. She had started her new life with Juan Carlos.

Part 3

Mark closed the apartment door after saying goodbye to Dionisio, and he locked it. He went to the kitchen to serve himself a glass of water without stop thinking about what Dionisio had told him about Claudia. Dionisio's story was very entertaining, but left Mark with the impression that Dionisio was hiding something important about her, he even thought for a second that the entire story probably was made up, but he put that thought aside. He concluded that it would have been best for Dionisio and Claudia to never have met, or maybe they used to be one person, attached to one another as Plato would suggest in the Origin of Love. Mark left the glass on the table, right on the edge of the kitchen counter. The door opened suddenly and violently letting a silhouette slither into the apartment, making Mark jump and hit the glass of water off the counter, the glass slowly fell the meter and a half separating the top of the counter and the kitchen floor, it was as if gravity had lost it power or time had slowed down. As it fell, the silhouette moving in real time was already in the kitchen holding a gun in his hand. The water reached the floor first splashing several areas while Mark's eyes grew as he saw what the silhouette had in his hand. When the glass reached the water on the floor, two sounds were heard, the glass shattering and the gun being fired against Mark's forehead. The bullet was fatal, making Mark collapse alongside the remains of the glass and the small pools of water that were now mixing with Mark's blood.

Dionisio found out about Mark's death the following day. He called him a few times but with no luck, and then decided to go check on him. When he arrived close to Mark's building, the police were already there. Dionisio learned what had happened from the downstairs neighbor that had heard the gunshot and then went to Mark's apartment to find him dead in his kitchen. Dionisio fainted as he heard these words, and when he came to, he was surrounded by policemen and paramedics. They asked him if he wanted them to take him home, to which Dionisio, by mere inertia, answered yes. The last thing he remembered about that day was himself in bed crying bitterly and blaming Claudia.

Salamanca's police questioned Dionisio a couple of times, but they never found anything that would link him to Mark's death; however, the detective in charge of the investigation concluded to himself that Dionisio was the murderer.

That was how The Death showed Dionisio that She was furious about him leaving La Costa. She showed him that she was still in charge. Her plan was to take him in La Costa but when the son of a bitch, as She called him, moved to a different city, She went to look for him. She hunted him, wrapping him slowly in Her darkness and loneliness. She was crushing him. Dionisio was thirty-four years old.

Part 4

When the sun finally illuminated the Diosdado's bedroom, Dionisio's mother felt an immense relief that the morning was breaking, after a night of insomnia. Beside her, her husband was still deeply asleep, ignoring an entire evening of his wife's tossing and tumbling. She had had problems sleeping ever since her son's last phone call revealing Salamanca as his new city. Mrs. Diosdado climbed down from bed, agitated and disturbing her husband's sleep; in reality she wanted him to wake up. She put her robe, went to the kitchen to prepare a very strong coffee to allow herself to be awake and face a new day under the shadow of her worries about her son and his decision to leave La Costa. She sat down for a few minutes to drink and enjoy the warmth of the coffee, and to confirm the thought inundating her mind: she would hire a private investigator to look for her son. She had no option, Dionisio gave her no option. He had not communicated with them and they were worried to death, especially when Melinda's disappearance was not exactly fresh but still in the air. Dionisio left La Costa like a thief leaves a house he had just robbed. The only thing his parents knew was that he was in Salamanca.

A few weeks after Dionisio's last phone conversation with them, the first thing his parents did was to go directly to his office to speak with whoever was in charge of the place. They entered the supervisor's office, made the required presentations and when the supervisor realized that they were Dionisio's parents he smiled. He asked them to sit down and asked how was Dionisio, to what Mrs. Diosdado replied that it was exactly what they had come to talk to him about. The supervisor was taken aback and worried, thinking that something bad had happened to Dionisio. The Diosdados, mostly the mother, told everything about Dionisio leaving La Costa some months back and that he had only communicated with them once from Salamanca. They wanted to know whether the supervisor knew of a telephone number or address that Dionisio might have left in case anyone from the office needed to contact him. The supervisor took a long breath and told the Diosdados that Dionisio came to see him one day to tell him that he was quitting without a reason. He left the company a few days later, leaving his office completely empty. There was no farewell party; he left without a trace. However, all the work he left was impeccable, clearly ordered and everything ready for his replacement. It was obvious that it took Dionisio a few weeks to leave everything ready at his work, it appeared that Dionisio had thought about quitting many weeks in advance. The meeting ended with the supervisor wishing the Diosdados the best of luck and hoping for them to get in contact with Dionisio soon. He reassured them that probably Dionisio was very busy and simply had not had the time to call them. Neither the supervisor nor the parents believed this last phrase.

Dionisio's parents' search for their son intensified and they were thankful that Mr. Diosdado had retired and had a lot of time on his hands. They contacted relatives and long forgotten friends living in Salamanca, but none of them could give them an indication of where Dionisio could be. However, they reassured the Diosdados that they would keep their eyes open and their ears attentive in case they heard any news.   Dionisio's parents travelled to Salamanca three times without any idea of how to start looking for him. The first two times, they drove around the city in a useless and absurd attempt to find him walking on the streets. When they discovered that this technique was not going to work in such a large city, they went back to La Costa with their hearts in their hands. A few weeks later, they went back with a better plan: they went to companies and institutions where Dionisio could have been working, however, this approach produced zero leads because no one in those places had heard of anyone with the name Dionisio Diosdado.

It was after these frustrating attempts that Mrs. Diosdado started to consider the idea of hiring a private investigator. She thought about the one El Negro Legorrea had hired to find Melinda, but he was too expensive for the Diosdados' budget. She found a significant number of private investigators in the yellow pages, narrowing her search to a few that sounded decent. She finally decided on someone named Juan de Dios, thinking that someone with such a divine last name must be someone of a positive reputation. That morning when she woke up from her sleepless night, she waited for her husband to wake up and for the clock to ring nine in the morning, a time that she thought was appropriate to call Juan de Dios' office. With a deep voice that inspired confidence,

Juan de Dios answered the phone to find Mrs. Diosdado on the other end of the line. After the usual salutations, Mrs. Diosdado explained with detail about her son's disappearance while Juan de Dios just made some affirmative noises. Then, it was Juan de Dios' turn to speak; he was very brief and basically only asked some exploratory questions. At the end, they agreed to meet at the private investigator's office at noon on the following day. The office was located in a small room in the basement of a twenty-story building located at the edge of La Costa in a very unkempt area of the city. Juan de Dios was a man of short stature with a marshmallow looking face, very dark browned skin and very professional and proud of his work. With a preemptive seriousness, he invited them into his office, encouraged them to sit down on two very comfortable brown leather chairs, and asked them if they wanted some coffee. Neither of the Diosdados accepted the drink.

"Tell me about your son…Dionisio, correct?" asked Juan de Dios while he grabbed a pen and a little notepad to take notes.

"Yes, Dionisio," answered Mrs. Diosdado. with some urgency in her voice.

Juan de Dios nodded.

"My wife already mentioned to you yesterday," interrupted Mr. Diosdado. "that Dionisio left to Salamanca without notice. The last time he contacted us was by phone, somewhere in the middle of March. We thought that he was going to call us again, but he hasn't. And look, it's been several months now and we know nothing about him."

"What was your son's profession here in La Costa?"

"He was a data analyst working for a laboratory in a clinic, on the Boulevard del Mar. He had worked there for at least three years, I guess. We already talked to his supervisor, he said that Dionisio left very quickly but left everything in impeccable order, but had no idea about his whereabouts."

"Does your son have enemies? Debts?"

"Not that we are aware of, in reality Dionisio has always been a very quiet and shy person, I doubt with his personality he has made enemies. And about debts, Dionisio made very good money, and as far as I know, he likes to save every single cent."

"Girlfriends? Close friends?"

"We…" Both parents looked at each other in doubt, "never met many of his friends. Sometimes he would talk about work colleagues, but we don't think he had a girlfriend. That is something that had always worried us, we never saw him with the idea or the mood to settle down. The only lady friend of his we knew, and he liked her, was Melinda Ramsden, but…"

"Melinda Ramsden? The one that disappeared?" interrupted Juan de Dios, with intense curiosity.

"Yes, the same." answered Mr. Diosdado.

"Let's elaborate, tell me, how is that Dionisio knew Melinda Ramsden?"

"My wife and I hosted her when, by a mere accident, I fractured her arm." Mr. Diosdado appeared embarrassed, "when I fell on her while walking on the beach – I was distracted, ok?" he justified himself, "I took her to the hospital, then to her apartment to find out that she was living in very precarious conditions and decided to take her to our home to live with us until she could afford something better…I mean, I broke her arm, that was the least I could do for her, right?"

Mrs. Diosdado just nodded and a tear came out, thinking about Melinda.

"I'm guessing that you," directing his question towards Mrs. Diosdado, "had no reservations that your husband brought a young lady to live in your house?"

"You police men are all the same. I've been asked this same question many times since Melinda's disappearance," answered Mrs. Diosdado, very upset, "and the answer is no, it did not bother me that Melinda lived with us; it was a very noble thing my husband did."

"My apologies, ma'am, my intentions were not to offend you, I am only trying to understand the situation. Please continue, Mr. Diosdado."

"Dionisio met Melinda, as you can imagine, through us. They went out a couple of times, and I guess they had a good time. We thought that those two had some future together, but El Negro Legorrea got in the way, and then Melinda disappeared."

"Of course, El Negro Legorrea, I knew that from the news but I don't remember yourselves or Dionisio being mentioned," interrupted Juan de Dios, as if saying that he already knew that part of the story.

"We were interviewed a couple of times, but it was never aired since all of the attention was directed to El Negro Legorrea." mentioned Mrs. Diosdado.

"Don't you think it's interesting that Melinda *and* Dionisio are missing?" asked Juan de Dios, probing them.

"Maybe," answered Mrs. Diosdado, feeling a little nervous and shifting in her chair, "it is something my husband and I have talked about, but Melinda disappeared months before Dionisio."

"If they are together, disappearing at different time points would be less suspicious," said Juan de Dios, as if he had resolved the case.

"It could be, but my maternal intuition tells me that that's not the case. I would have loved to see my son and Melinda together, but it was obvious there was not a true spark between the two of them. And of course, El Negro Legorrea showed up."

"It's just a theory, but let's proceed with the details of your son's life. Did Dionisio live with you?"

"No, he lived in an apartment that he originally rented from us, then we told him that the apartment was his, but still gave us some money every month to pay the rent until one day he didn't, but we never asked him why, we just supposed he decided not to do so." answered Mr. Diosdado.

"What happened to the apartment now that he is gone?"
Mr. Diosdado thought for a second.

"I assume that it may be rented to someone. Dionisio mentioned the last time he called that he had taken care of everything before leaving La Costa."

"So, there may be someone living in the apartment, someone that may be paying Dionisio rent on a regular basis? Have you visited the apartment to talk to whoever may be living there?"

The Diosdados' eyes shone for the first time in a long time, there was a shred of hope in what Juan de Dios had just said, and at the same time, they felt incredibly stupid for not thinking before about the possibility that someone was renting the apartment.

"No, we haven't been there, we should have gone!" pleaded Mrs. Diosdado towards Mr. Diosdado.

"And so, what are we waiting for? Let's go to see what we can found out." interrupted Juan de Dios.

They stood up, Juan de Dios grabbed his notepad and the three of them left.

Mr. Diosdado knocked a few times on the apartment door, but no one opened. They waited, looking at each other and asking in silence what to do when a woman, a neighbor, came out from the elevator with a few supermarket bags hanging from her arms. Juan de Dios stopped her, greeted her and asked her if she knew anything about the person living in the apartment, pointing at Dionisio's door. The lady looked at the three of them suspiciously but told them that it had been a while since she last saw the young man living there, and that she had not heard any noise coming out of the apartment. Juan de Dios thanked her, and the lady disappeared quickly into her apartment.

"Is there a chance you have a key to the apartment?"

"Yes, I always keep a copy in my car's glove compartment. Do you think we should get in?" asked Mr. Diosdado with considerable doubt.

"Well, it appears that no one lives there, according to the neighbor, and therefore it is still your son's residency, giving you the right to go inside, especially under the current circumstances."

Before opening the door, they knocked a few times again, waiting for an answer that never came. Mr. Diosdado opened the door and the three of them entered cautiously as if they were breaking and entering an unknown person's home. The smell of humidity was intense and the air inside was stagnant, it was obvious that the apartment had not been opened in a long time. Mrs. Diosdado said an '*oh my God*' as she went to the window to open it and get some air circulation. Juan de Dios saw her intentions, but stopped her, telling her that for the moment it was better to leave everything untouched. Mrs. Diosdado did not accept the comment, said that the smell was horrible, and concluded that opening a window would not influence finding her son. Thinking that she had won the argument, she proceeded to open the window.

The apartment was impeccable, with the exception of the smell and the dust covering most surfaces. In Dionisio's room, all was in order and the closets were full of Dionisio's clothes as were the dresser drawers. It looked as if Dionisio had suddenly disappeared. After inspecting the apartment completely, they realized that there was nothing there that could indicate why Dionisio left or where in Salamanca he was.

"I am sorry, but here there is not a clue about your son's whereabouts, and it is obvious he did not take anything with him. Is there another place that Dionisio would visit with frequency?" asked Juan de Dios, realizing that his best lead had dissolved.

"Not that we know of."

Silence.

"Let's think for a minute, maybe we are missing something important. Can you take me to where your son used to work? I would like to talk to his supervisor."

Mrs. Diosdado closed the windows, telling her husband that she would come tomorrow to open them again and dust the furniture. Mr. Diosdado nodded. They left the apartment and once in the elevator, Juan de Dios pressed the lobby's button noticing that there was an extra button without a floor number at the top of all the others. Juan de Dios asked what the button was for, and Mr. Diosdado answered that it was for the roof, where there were some little rooms.

"What little rooms?" Juan de Dios asked.

"Each apartment has a little room on the roof, it could be used as a storage or extra room."

"Do you think we can go to that little room?"

"I suppose so, the apartment's key opens the room, too."

They reached the lobby, but no one got out of the elevator. Juan de Dios pressed the numberless button. A very bright sun welcomed them to the roof, contrasting with the darkness of the little room. They entered, and Mr. Diosdado turned the light on.

Part 5

The days were beautiful, everything looked crystalized due to the sun reflecting on the little drops of rain that had fallen during midday on the trees, benches, and cars. The parks were full of people walking and enjoying the weather and life. That was what Dionisio could see from his apartment's window. Mark had died three months ago, the exact time that Dionisio had spent, mostly, inside his apartment. Obviously, he would go out to buy his necessities, but would come back inside as if a phobia for the outside had invaded his body. The days for him were lethargic and overwhelmingly slow, time was a heavy weight over his back: the minutes would cram and the hours would spill over him, turning his life into a voluntary prison where Dionisio had decided to die. But of course, The Death, in the meantime, had other plans.

He was there, in that small, unkempt and dusty apartment that Dionisio rented from a woman with a very long face, like a stick, living in the first floor. He did not care about the condition of the apartment, and he was not going to clean it. His savings were running out; he miscalculated how much money he would have needed to survive, and now he realized that very soon he would have to vacate the apartment and find somewhere else to live, and somewhere much more affordable, which was going to be hard. He let his beard and hair grow, and the lack of proper nourishment made him lose weight, so much that his body looked like an ambulant skeleton, as if he were a concentration camp prisoner. He would spend his days sitting at the edge of his bed, or on the chair close to the table, or beside the window, longing and waiting for The Death to arrive and put him out of his misery as soon as possible. But She was torturing him, just for spite.

Part 6

The interior of the little room on the roof had a small desk and a very old-looking and uncomfortable chair. There were stacks of paper covering most of the surface of the desk, most of them of the same height. On the floor, there were many cardboard boxes of different sizes, all of them closed. Dionisio's dad approached the desk and realized that something was written by hand on the sheets of paper, it was his son's handwriting. He sat on the chair, uncomfortably and without minding the other two people in the room, and started browsing through the sheets. Juan de Dios crouched to see the content of some of the boxes. He opened one close to where Mrs. Diosdado was standing and to their surprise, he pulled out women's wigs of different colors. He opened another box finding skirts, blouses, panties and other women's clothing items. Mrs. Diosdado crouched to open one box, she found shoes and more women's clothes. Juan de Dios proceeded to move some boxes that were stacked on top of each other and found that there was a long rectangular mirror leaning on the wall, hidden behind the stacked boxes. On the top of the mirror there was something written in black with cursive and very elegant font, like calligraphy. It was a name: Claudia.

Mr. Diosdado was focused reading the paper sheets and had not noticed that his wife and Juan de Dios had opened all of the boxes. When he finally looked at them, his eyes were alarmed about the contents. Without saying a word, he pointed to the sheets of paper.

Part 7

His breathing was loud and resonated in all the room. His chest hurt, a pain that stunk of death, and his body exuded a bitter odor. His life, or whatever remained of it, was an absurdity, a cruelty. The Death had made him a prisoner of himself, of his mind, of his body. She would touch his heart, just to make it fail, and when Dionisio would think it was the end, She, The Disgraceful, would remove Her fingers off it to grant him more life. The Death had swallowed all memory from his former life, of his parents, of his work. We could not recognize himself, and sometimes he would think that it was only a mirage or the result of someone else's imagination, a very cruel someone. He was alone, in the middle of his solitude, surrounded by darkness; there was not hope, no light, no road to follow.

Before leaving La Costa, Dionisio made a transference of his savings to a bank account in Salamanca with the precise instructions to the bank to deny information to anyone that may ask for personal information about him. The great majority of his money was left in the La Costa bank where he had added his parents as beneficiaries. He also instructed the bank to send a letter to his parents on a predetermined date in the future to let them know about the existence of this account. The money he had transferred to Salamanca was almost completely out. He came down the stairs from his apartment, weak, with a foggy mind, and shaking. He arrived to the stick-faced landlady's apartment, and knocked on the door from where she came out almost instantly, as if she were waiting for him. She looked at him with disgust, and who could blame her, the man in front of her stunk like microwaved garbage. They exchange a few words, but the stick-face lady was unemphatic and definite: no money, no apartment.

Dionisio returned to his room to think about the possibilities, but the truth was clear: he would have to leave the apartment to live, maybe, in a shelter, until The Death would come to get him. The end of the month came and with that his last day in the apartment, he picked up whatever he had decided to take with him and left indifferently from that place that for many days he had called his home. Once on the street, he put on his jacket, breathed deeply, and faced his first moments as a homeless person. The happiness of Salamanca's streets is hidden to those that have nowhere to go. To him, the streets were painted of gray and solitude, despite the hundreds of people walking along them. People would avoid getting too close to him because his body smelled as if he were already decomposing. Close to him was The Death, enjoying every single moment of his suffering. He knew it, he had seen Her several times when he turned his head to snoop quickly. *Why do you torment me? What have I done to you? I just asked for a little more of life to make fun of the doctor helping my mom give birth, I wanted to prove his knowledge wrong, to let him know that he was not going to say when I live or when I die; why did you not take the doctor right there? He was playing the role of You! You have won, leave me in peace! No… no. Instead, take me now, let this punishment end! But You will not do it, You, Disgraceful! You are laughing at me! Yeah, always your pawn, and this is how you play me? Tell me, what have I done to you?"*

She remained quiet and just stood there, watching him, thinking.

Part 8

'Claudia lived all her childhood in Salamanca…' read the sheet of paper numbered *1* in Mr. Diosdado's hand, resembling the beginning of a story, maybe a fairy tale or something like that. When he had finished with that sheet, he handed it to his wife, and when she was done reading it, she gave it to Juan de Dios. They were concentrated in reading those sheets that started to form a narrative that Dionisio had written, that to them appeared to be something that he had made up. Juan de Dios was tired of reading about Claudia Alicante's life, which was written with a great amount of detail, and so he decided to browse other sheets of paper from other stacks. All of them still narrated Claudia Alicante's life but what caught Juan de Dios' attention was that every so often, the name Dionisio Diosdado would appear in dialogues with Claudia Alicante. Juan de Dios asked the Diosdados if they knew anyone named Claudia Alicante, and they quickly answered, without taking their eyes off the sheets they were holding, that they have never heard that name before. Juan de Dios lost interest in the sheets of paper, left the ones in his hand on the column where he had taken them and when he moved his elbow he hit an adjacent column that started to tilt; he hurried,

clumsily, to stop the column from falling, but the movement caused the column to speed its collapse, spreading sheets of paper all over the floor. He cursed in silence and knelt to pick up the papers while the Diosdados looked at him in disbelief. Both knelt to help him. Mrs. Diosdado picked up one sheet at random, recognizing the name of Melinda Ramsden written on it. She stopped and started reading out loud the contents of the sheet. Mr. Diosdado and Juan de Dios stood up when they heard the name of the British girl.

At the beginning, the narrative told the story of the origin of Melinda and her adventures in South America, exactly as she had told the Diosdados about them. Juan de Dios asked Mrs. Diosdado to skip a few paragraphs, she obeyed and they heard how Melinda had arrived to La Costa and had met the Diosdados. The narrative was interrupted by conversations between Dionisio and Claudia, in which Claudia chastised Dionisio that he had forgotten her because of that British woman, and Dionisio would defend himself by saying that there was nothing between them. Mrs. Diosdado reached the end of that sheet of paper, looked at the page number reading *75* and knelt to find the next one. She found it, and without standing she proceed to read it. Mr. Diosdado and Juan de Dios were completely absorbed by the narrative. Then, she stopped reading out loud and read in silence to herself, her eyes turned wet and she was breathing hard; the sheet that she was holding dropped to the floor.

What happened? shouted Mr. Diosdado franticly. Juan de Dios took the paper sheet numbered *76* and read it to himself. Page 76 described how Melinda Ramsden was thrown off a cliff by The Death, disguised as Claudia Alicante.

Part 9

He cursed himself for not finding out in advance the address of the shelter for homeless people. He had absolutely no idea where it might be, causing him to spend the first night sleeping on the street. He tried to shelter himself in a small nook formed by the stairs of an apartment building, but the night guard saw him and shooed him away as if he were a stray dog. Dionisio stood up and left both in shame and with complete lack of faith in humanity from the way he had been treated. However, he thought that if he were in the night guard's shoes, he would have done the same. He walked the darkness of the night for one or two hours, cold and hungry. Without noticing, he had arrived to the park where he had met Mark. He sat on a bench to see the emptiness of the park. He closed his eyes and fell asleep deeply. He did not dream.

The cold of the early morning woke him up. His muscles were stiff because of the hardness of the bench. He tried to think what he was doing on a bench at the park, and it was at this moment that his mind brought him to his miserable reality. He walked to a big oak tree to relief himself from urine and feces. When he was done, he took his belongings to walk to a non-working three-level fountain still full of water. He splashed cold water onto his face and cleaned himself the best he could under the circumstances. His stomach hurt of hunger. He searched his front pocket to find a small plastic bag with a few coins and bills, enough to barely survive for a few days. He came back to the bench to think what he was going to do and to wait for the stores to open to buy some bread and a coffee. He thought, but his mind landed on a feeling of uselessness and frustration. She used to have a roof above his head, and a good one in La Costa. He took his hands to his face and started a bitter weep that no one heard.

When he finally started walking, he found a small store that had just opened its doors. Before he could walk inside, the clerk came out to tell him that he could not get into the store in those conditions, but before sending him back to the street, as a humanitarian gesture, he gave Dionisio a quart of milk and a few orange-flavored pastries. Dionisio offered some money but the clerk told him to save it for a rainy day. Dionisio smiled at and thanked him many times. He walked a few blocks and when he found a place that appeared adequate to have breakfast, he sat on the sidewalk, resting his back on a house wall. The milk and pastries tasted like heaven to him, even more because the sun had come out and caressed his face with tenderness. The heat of the sun and the food comforted his soul and body.

He finished his breakfast and stood up, determined to find the homeless shelter. He walked towards the city's downtown, finding on his way two men in a similar condition to his: one of them with a long and unkempt beard, dirty clothes, and looked to be about fifty years old; the other one was younger and looked in better condition. Both of them were sitting at the edge of the sidewalk arguing angrily. He got closer with some fear and shyness, greeted them clumsily, and asked them about the shelter's address. Both men looked at him with contempt and threatening eyes but did not answer the question. They returned to the argument Dionisio had interrupted. Dionisio tried asking them one more time and after he finished, the long-bearded man stood up and very angrily answered him to go fuck himself. Dionisio jumped backwards and left quickly trembling.

He turned the corner and found another homeless who immediately asked Dionisio for money while grabbing his jacket. Dionisio shook him off, running away from him as fast as he could. He reached a small park, sat on a bench where he lowered his head to cry about his miserable condition, and asked The Death to take him once and for all. The people walking by heard his words and thought he was crazy. All ignored him.

Sister Sotomayor was a young woman of around eighteen or twenty years old, recently accepted into one of the two convents in Salamanca. Her torso was thin, ending in voluptuous hips that made her look like a bell under her nun's attire. Her hair was long and black, hidden behind the white hat that she always wore. Her eyes distilled mercy and her soft passive voice could heal a thousand illnesses. Sister Sotomayor found Dionisio while he was weeping bitterly on the park bench. She approached him and with her angelical voice addressed him as *my little child,* asking him for his name. Dionisio took his face away from his hands to find the origin of that beautiful voice, finding God's eyes looking at him. Without hesitation, he said his name was Dionisio, Dionisio Diosdado. *Where do you live*? was the next question. Dionisio just shook his head. *Come with me, I will take you to the shelter where the nuns will take good care of you as long as you need it.* Dionisio, as a little child, obeyed without saying a word, following that heavenly soul that had found him.

The shelter was part of the convent, which was associated with the church of the Holiest Mercy and was attended mostly by the nuns living there. The architecture was colonial and looked like an enormous hacienda in the middle of the city. Sister

Sotomayor took him to a small room where the register was. There was a nun behind a very old desk sitting on a small wooden chair as old as the desk; she asked for his personal information and took note of his possessions. Then, she asked Dionisio to leave all his things with her and invited him to take a shower. *Shower?* asked Dionisio with curiosity. The sister behind the desk nodded and asked Sister Sotomayor to show him the way. They entered a long hallway paved with semi polished rocks and flanked by several rooms full of bunk beds where many men rested, read and played cards. Dionisio saw himself reflected in them. They walked a bit more to a door leading to the showers. Sister Sotomayor asked him to enter, undress and place his clothes in one of the plastic bags he would find inside.

"Why?" He asked.

"Because they will be washed and you will find some clothes to use on the shelves inside the room."

Dionisio nodded as he entered the room. He showered with really warm comfortable water and dressed himself with clothes that were at least a couple of sizes too large. His starved body was fresh and clean; he felt alive. He came out of the room with the plastic bag containing his clothes to find sister Sotomayor waiting for him with divine patience. She took the bag and told him to follow her to one of the rooms. They entered one with five bunk beds and two individual beds; the sun filtered through a large window making the room feel warm. It smelled clean. Sister Sotomayor greeted every one of the residents in the room while walking to the bed Dionisio would occupy.

-"The afternoon meal is at two and you can pick up your belongings any time you want in the room where you registered" said the Sister. "Father

Rigoberto will make his rounds around noon and would love to talk to you.

She bowed her head softly and said her goodbyes. Dionisio thanked her sincerely.

Part 10

"Before we reach a conclusion that we do not know with certainty, I believe we need to consider the possibilities and find more clues that may indicate to us where Dionisio may be, and also the reason for the things we just found inside." said Juan de Dios outside the little room while the sun was hitting his face.

"Of course." answered Dionisio's father, while Mrs. Diosdado looked at the horizon searching for an answer or an explanation to the many things she did not understand.

"I don't think your son had anything to do with Melinda's death; what we read could very well be just something he came up with. Right now, that is something we should not worry about. I'd suggest to not take anything outside the little room but, whenever you have time, it'd be important for you to finish reading the papers for any possible clue. Maybe there's an address in Salamanca or at least a reference point. In the meantime, I will try to find out who Claudia Alicante is, if she is real or not. If she is, then she may be able to help us find your son."

The Diosdados nodded without saying a word to Juan de Dios. He said his goodbyes and told them that in a few days he would contact them. Mr. and Mrs. Diosdado looked at each other in silence, and after a brief pause, they entered the room to read what they now realized was a handwritten manuscript.

The hundreds of sheets of paper they found were read with a lot of curiosity during the afternoon and night of that same day. When they finished, they were confused and full of questions, but mostly they were sweating in fear.

They did not wait for Juan de Dios to reach them to make the next move. The very next day they left to Dionisio's former place of work. They parked just in front of the building, got out of the car, and stood watching in the direction of the bridge connecting the two towers. He counted the floors to reach the conclusion that his son's former office was on the same floor as the bridge. They took the elevator, turned right then left, and after a brief hesitation they took another right. They could not find the entrance to the bridge. Mr. Diosdado looked through a window and realized they were one floor above the bridge. They took the emergency stairs to descend one floor, when they opened the door, the entrance of the bridge was right in front of them. The view of the ocean was incredible and mesmerizing. Dionisio's mother took her husband's hand and for an instant they felt their son's presence. They crossed the bridge to find an identical building to the one where Dionisio's office used to be, full of doors leading to offices. Mr. Diosdado entered the first one and asked a fat man sitting in front of a computer if he knew someone named Claudia Alicante. The fat man looked at him suspiciously and answered that he had never heard such a name. They tried their luck in a couple more offices without a positive outcome. They stood in the hallway thinking what to do while a very beautiful woman walked past them, she saw them lost and turned around to ask them if there was something she could help them with. Mr. Diosdado told her they were looking for Claudia Alicante but they did not know the floor or office where she worked. The beautiful lady smiled and asked them to follow her. They passed several doors until she stopped in front of one, it was a waiting room. There was a telephone on a table that the beautiful lady took and dialed nine, someone answered on the other side and she asked for Claudia Alicante. There was a pause and the beautiful lady ended the call with a thank you. *Her office is on the next floor, room 819*, said the beautiful lady with a satisfactory smile. They thanked her and left promptly to the emergency stairs.

The next floor was an identical copy of the previous floor. They walked along the hallway following the numbering on the doors until they found the 819. They knocked on the door and when there was no answer, they decided to enter. Inside there was a sea of desks with computers on them and some offices on the sides. People were working and paid no attention to the couple standing there. They approached a well-dressed lady with very white skin and red hair, for sure she was a foreigner. Mr. Diosdado asked her for Claudia Alicante. The red-headed lady looked at them without any emotion and answered that the engineer was on vacation, on her belated honeymoon, and she would come back next week. Dionisio's parents decided not to leave Claudia Alicante a message, and they cordially thanked her and left. Before leaving that place, Mr. Diosdado turned around and asked the red-headed lady the name of Claudia's husband. Juan Carlos Tilapia, she answered.

Part 11

When Dionisio woke up, he found father Rigoberto's eyes looking at him. A tall man with wrinkled, life-seasoned face, and a very white smile with impeccable teeth. Father Rigoberto indicated Dionisio with a hand gesture not to rise from the bed. Dionisio sort of sat up greeting him. Father Rigoberto introduced himself and offered peace while extending his hand to shake Dionisio's. The father asked him if the sisters had treated him well and whether he had eaten anything. Dionisio answered yes to both questions. Father Rigoberto looked at him, smiled, and sat at the edge of the bed. Dionisio, clumsily and a bit uncomfortable, moved his legs to make more room for father Rigoberto to sit down. Father Rigoberto indicated to Dionisio that the sisters of the convent would treat him very well as long as he needed, but recommended Dionisio to find a job that would allow him to make some money to start a new life, and why not, maybe even rent a small apartment at the edge of the city. Dionisio just nodded to everything the father Rigoberto said without letting him know that he did not want to start a new life. He was at the end of his. Father Rigoberto stood up, said goodbye by shaking his hand and asked him to look for him if he needed anything.

Dionisio got off from bed and after putting on his recently washed clothes, left the convent to walk the streets of Salamanca. The sun was bright and its heat warmed his bones. He walked for a couple of blocks without a place to go, and at some point, he stood in front of a bridal shop full of wedding dresses. He looked at the dresses with sparkly eyes and for a moment, his mind took him to paths of his past where he saw Claudia wearing one of them. He imagined her with a big smile behind a white veil while walking slowly to the church's altar, where Juan Carlos, with an even bigger smile, waited anxiously. When she arrived to him, a sharp pain crossed Dionisio's heart.

He fell to the ground as an inanimate object, his breathing was arduous and his face full of sun rays. He felt himself dying. He closed his eyes to wait for the long-expected moment and when he did it, he felt an unexpected peace crawling up and warming up his body in a kindly way. He smiled, thinking that dying was not as tragic as he had expected it to be, and let himself be overcome by a feeling of peace that flooded his body. A familiar voice called his name, asking him to open his eyes. When he did, he found the comforting eyes of sister Sotomayor who was softly rubbing Dionisio's forehead with her hand. Dionisio stood precariously, the pain had passed and he let himself be taken directly to the shelter by sister Sotomayor. When they were in the shelter's room, sister Sotomayor instructed Dionisio that the best thing to do was to rest and to nourish his body well before trying to go out to the streets again. Dionisio agreed and sister Sotomayor left the room as if she were hovering a few inches above the ground.

Dionisio spent a few days without leaving the shelter. He would eat at the established hours and avoided any type of conversation with the other residents. He also spent his time reading books that the sisters left on a small bookshelf beside the entrance to the dormitory. He read a couple of novels and nonfiction books which helped him to free his mind of the many thoughts rushing through it. However, the only activity that he looked forward to was the daily hour in which Father Rigoberto would sit on a bench located in a small garden at the back of the shelter to tell stories about his life. Most nuns and homeless would gather to hear Father Rigoberto, and sometime Sister Sotomayor would bring her camera and take a few pictures to have a record of the occasion. During these gatherings, Dionisio found out that Father Rigoberto was born in a small town in northern Italy during the big war. His parents were arrested by the fascists in power and he was taken to an orphanage which was managed by some nuns. The orphanage was part of a convent, localized on top of a small hill outside of town. He was three months old. Father Rigoberto never saw his parents again. He liked to study, and the many books he read were his best friends during his childhood years. He would get lost in their stories and they made him fantasize with adventures that he would take once he would become emancipated and leave the orphanage. This happened when he turned eighteen. The nuns sat with him one morning to explained to him that it was time for him to leave the orphanage and make a life, a good one, in the outside world. The young Rigoberto felt some sadness but at the same time he was excited about starting a new life for himself. The nuns gave him some money, cried, and hugged their goodbyes. They also asked him what was going to be his last name because he would need one in the outside world. It was true, his parents never mentioned his last name and he grew up thinking of himself as just Rigoberto. He thought for a minute, he left the room to quickly grab a book from his belongings to read the cover. He came back and told the nuns: Verne, Rigoberto Verne.

Rigoberto Verne made his way to the south of Italy where he worked and spent his days and night working for a fishing boat. He saved a small sum of money which he used to travel to north Africa. He arrived in Morocco where he lived for two years working as a clay potter and pretending to be a Muslim. One afternoon, while walking alone outside of town and under the heavy sun, a 'snake of destiny', as he called it, bit his ankle, injecting its venom into his leg. Rigoberto Verne was practically dying when he arrived into town where he stumbled upon a young Spanish physician with a big wooden cross hanging from his neck. This physician saw Rigoberto Verne's condition and recognized his symptoms. He quickly helped him and by some unknown miracle, saved his life. The Spanish physician cared for him during the recovery period and the two became very good friends. The Spanish physician asked Rigoberto Verne to travel with him to Malaga just for a few days to help him work at a small clinic. He went and the few days turned into twenty years where Rigoberto Verne worked in any job he could find, he fell in love with the beautiful Spaniard women, and had a great time. However, inside of him there was something missing. One fall morning, while walking in the streets of Malaga, Rigoberto Verne realized that a building he had walked by many times was a monastery. He looked through the fence to see the monks and a light went on inside of him: he realized at that very moment that his life's purpose was the holy sanctity. He tried many times to join the monastery, but every time he was rejected for reasons he did not understand. When he was about to quit trying to become a monk, and while having a cup of coffee and reading the newspaper in a small café, a shadow approached him asking him how the country was, to which Rigoberto Verne, without taking his eyes out of the newspaper answered *'like shit'*. He finally looked up to find a tall blue-eyed man dressed as a Catholic priest. Father Antón asked permission to sit on the empty chair while asking him more questions about the news of the day. They talked for many hours and at some point in the conversation, Rigoberto Verne told Father Antón about his desire to become a monk. Father

Antón smiled and asked him what were his reasons
for that desire. Rigoberto Verne answered that he
could not describe it, but he knew that it was his
destiny. They said their goodbyes and Father Antón
gave him his address, if he ever wanted to meet to
discuss more about his future. And Rigoberto Verne
did. Two years after this conversation, Rigoberto
Verne was ordained as a Catholic priest.

He traveled to many places teaching, helping,
and spreading his religion to all people wanting or not
wanting to listen to him. He would go back to Spain to
spend Christmas there in the company of all the
people he considered as family: the Spanish
physician and Father Antón. In one of his trips, he
ended up in Salamanca, on another continent. He fell
in love with the city's colonial style sprinkled with
many colors and joyful gentle people. From that
moment, he established himself in Salamanca and
never returned to Spain, not even for Christmas.

"If you want, tell me something about you."
"There's not much to say, Father. I was born
here in Salamanca but lived most of my life in La
Costa. And now I am back."
Father Rigoberto smiled with love.
"I see, but tell me about your family."
"My parents are still in La Costa, but I'd rather
not talk about them."
"You are very young and very smart to be in a
shelter. Has life treated you bad?"
"No Father, it was a personal decision."
"Do not tell me you want to become a priest."
"No Father, I couldn't. It isn't for me."
"Leaving everything behind is quite a decision.
You must have a deep reason to do so.
"You are not wrong, Father."

Part 12

"It turns out there is indeed a Claudia Alicante." mentioned Juan de Dios through the telephone, "and I know exactly where she lives."

"Yes, we already found out that she exists." answered Dionisio's father, almost proud.

"How do you know that?" asked Juan de Dios, surprised.

"We decided to go to our son's former place of work and tried to find her there, but we couldn't because she is on her honeymoon."

"Ok, that is important information," added Juan de Dios, a bit offended that they had not revealed this piece of evidence sooner, "I would like to visit Claudia Alicante at her home when she comes back. But, until that time, I would like to take another look at the manuscript your son wrote to see if I can find some sort of additional clues. Do you think I can have access to the small room?"

The following day, early in the morning, private investigator Juan de Dios was sitting reading Dionisio's manuscript. He had a little notebook where every now and then he would write names, descriptions, and other details he considered to be important. When the night arrived of that same day, Juan de Dios was finishing reading the entire manuscript. At the end, he turned almost unwillingly to the mirror in the room, and when he saw himself, he felt a presence staring back at him. He felt an irrational fear. He closed his little notebook and left the little room as soon as possible.

One week later, Juan de Dios called the Diosdados once more. During that conversation, he found out that Dionisio's parents had decided to do nothing until they heard back from the detective. He thanked them and told them that he had important information and wanted to talk to them in person that same afternoon. At four o'clock of that cloudy and suffocating summer day, Juan de Dios entered the Diosdados' home with a serious and worrisome expression. Mrs. Diosdado offered him tea or coffee which he rejected, but instead asked for a glass of water with a lot of ice.

"Look," started Juan de Dios calmly, as if he were about to teach a class, "if Claudia Alicante exists, I thought, then maybe other people that are mentioned in your son's manuscript are also real, and so the possibility exists that they may know where your son is. Therefore, I decided to write down some of the names and try to match them in a computer program linked to the police and other government reports in the country."

Dionisio's parents looked at him intensely without interrupting him, but their faces were already full of a thousand questions.

"Some of the names match people from many regions of the country, but I found them irrelevant for our purposes, according to my experience." Juan de Dios paused for questions that were not asked, "However, there are names that did match people from Salamanca, Monserrat, and La Costa, some of which I think are of extreme relevance.

"What do you mean?" interrupted Mr. Diosdado.

"Melinda Ramsden, Joaquín Villagrán, Rómulo Ramirez and Alfonso Murieta…" Juan the Dios hesitated, "…are all dead, well of course, with the exception of Melinda Ramsden, as we do not know for sure what happened to her. The most incredible

part, and this is where this case turns…delicate, is the fact that the way Joaquín Villagrán and Rómulo Ramírez died happened *exactly* as Dionisio had described it in his manuscript. Also, the age that they were when they passed away was similar to what we can deduct from Dionisio's writing." There was a long uncomfortable pause.
Dionisio's mother started to cry while her husband tried to console her.

"Who are these people? I have never even heard of them." said Mr. Diosdado.

"Alfonso Murieta was killed while he was finishing high school, according to the police record, because a fight probably caused by a woman. But no one was charged. He was in the same high school as your son, school number 68, correct?"

"Are you trying to tell me," Dionisio's dad raised from his chair as if he was ready to fight, "that my son killed all these people? Dionisio is a decent person that would not hurt anyone! We hired you to find him, not to charge my son with ridiculous crimes!"

"I didn't say that," answered Juan de Dios, somewhat scared but in a calm tone.

"Then what the *fuck* are you trying to say!?"

"I really…I really don't know. But I find it very interesting that Dionisio tells about these people and the way they died. Maybe he just read about these people somewhere and decided to use them in his writing."

Dionisio's father was now pacing the room from one side to the other.

"Mr. Diosdado, we are not going to draw conclusions from things we know nothing about. We'll wait for Claudia Alicante to come back from her honeymoon and then we can ask her about your son."

Juan de Dios stood up, took his belongings, had one last long sip of the icy water and rapidly said goodbye. Dionisio's parents looked at each other under a cloud of questions and doubt.

Part 13

The emergency services left in a rush when they received Mrs. Remedio's phone call asking for help. She woke up as she had done every single for the past several years: she prepared breakfast, woke up her kids, and opened the front door to get the newspaper thrown at one of the three entry steps to give it to her husband. However, that day, when she mechanically opened the front door, she not only found the newspaper but also a disgusting smell coming out from something lying on one of the steps. She expelled a small and ridiculous scream as if someone had pinched her buttocks. When Mrs. Remedios looked carefully she realized that the something was a man, a sleeping man, probably a homeless. She immediately closed the door, went to the kitchen, grabbed the broom and went back to the door. The man was still there. With the broomstick and from as far as possible, Mrs. Remedios touched the man's side. He did not move. She repeated touching him but this time with more force, and again, the man did not move. The third time, she pushed him with more force, making the man roll down the steps onto the sidewalk. Still, he did not move, it was as if a sack of oranges had been thrown from the stairs. Mrs. Remedios expelled another ridiculous little scream and took her hands to her mouth as the universal sign for terror indicates. She closed and locked the door, grabbed the telephone and called emergency services. Seven minutes later, the paramedics were helping Dionisio. He was alive, barely, but needed to be treated immediately. They took him delicately inside the ambulance where they put in his arm an intravenous needle connected to saline solution to hydrate him, and in his nose, they connected tubes for oxygen coming from a small tank. They took him to the General Hospital of Salamanca. In the meantime, The Death, being already in Mrs. Remedios' house had decided to take her husband, maybe with a fulminant heart attack, but when She smelled the frying bacon Mrs. Remedios was preparing in the kitchen, She decided to stay and enjoy that delicious breakfast, which bought Mr. and Mrs. Remedios a long and prosperous life. They died past a hundred years of age.

The news spread like fire throughout the shelter: Father Rigoberto had been murdered in a dark alley close to the shelter. He had left to enjoy some free time the previous evening with friends that lived close by. He walked there and also on his way back. It was a beautiful cool clear night. He took a shortcut that led him to a dark alley but that did not concern him at all. At the end of the alley he could see the light of the shelter's side door. And that was the last thing he saw in life because immediately, a dexterous hand stabbed him fifteen times all over his body. Father Rigoberto Verne grabbed the cross hanging from his neck and collapsed to the ground violently, in pain, and bloody. He never saw who killed him that night.

Salamanca woke up to this horrible news. The reporters camped outside the shelter while the police tried to keep them away. Father Rigoberto Verne was mourned and cried over for forty days and forty nights, and his body was taken by ship back to Italy, where he was buried in a cemetery close to the orphanage where he was raised.

When he woke up in the middle of the night in the shelter, Dionisio felt The Death's stare looking at him from the edge of his bed. She was beautiful, more than ever, maybe because of the moon light reflecting on Her dried skin. Dionisio was not afraid, on the contrary, he felt relief. The Death nodded at him indicating it was time. Everybody else was deep asleep in the room. He stood up and tried to pick up some of his belongings, but She stopped him. He got out to the hallway, the shelter was in full peace and quiet. He walked making sure if She was following him. She was. She nodded again and Dionisio understood that he needed to exit the shelter. Carefully he opened the door that made no sound, as if it were made out of thin air. He got out to the street, the moon was beautiful and it projected his shadow onto the sidewalk. Her shadow was a few steps behind.

Part 14

"Good afternoon, may I speak with Miss Claudia Alicante?" asked Juan de Dios.
"This is she, but I am no longer Alicante, now I am Tilapia. What can I do for you?" answered Claudia as if trying to help this person.
"My name is Juan de Dios Agraciado and I'm a private investigator. This may sound strange to you, but I am trying to find a missing person, and I have some evidence, not confirmed, indicating that you may know something about him."
"My God, and who is this person?" answered a now concerned Claudia.

"If you don't mind, I'd rather have this conversation in person."

Three days later, Juan de Dios waited in a café located in the Boulevard del Mar. He sat comfortably while sipping an iced cappuccino under the shade of a big umbrella right on the side walk. Claudia Tilapia arrived on time to the meeting. She was well-dressed with a light blue blouse contrasting her fair skin color, and tight dark blue pants that exquisitely delineated her figure. Juan de Dios saw her and immediately thought that Claudia Tilapia was the real-life representation of Dionisio's description of Claudia Alicante.

Juan de Dios stood up to asked her if she was Claudia Alicante or now Tilapia. She smiled and answered yes. Juan de Dios introduced himself again and gave her a business card that she distractedly put inside her pocket. Juan de Dios asked her if she wanted something to drink, to which Claudia said that a cold soda would suffice. He ordered it. Juan de Dios went directly to the reason of their meeting. He told Claudia that he had been hired by Mr. and Mrs. Diosdado; he paused to study Claudia's facial expression after hearing their last name, but there was nothing unusual. He explained that they were looking for their son that had moved to Salamanca, but did not leave any details of how to contact him. The soda arrived and Claudia started drinking it and then asked for this missing person's name. *Dionisio Diosdado*, answered Juan de Dios, a little rushed. Claudia left the soda on the table, leaned on the back of the chair, sighed and crossed her arms looking at the Boulevard del Mar thinking or trying to remember something. Juan de Dios looked at her eyes and realized they were beautiful, thinking that anyone could get lost in them for an eternity. Claudia came back from her thinking to tell him that the name sounded familiar, especially because it is a unique name not easy to forget, but she could not remember who that person was, or is. Juan de Dios told her that Dionisio worked in the tower next to hers, and it was at that moment that Claudia's memory came back.

"Of course!" she exclaimed, and smiled big as if she had discovered something very important. Claudia told Juan de Dios that she used to cross the bridge connecting both towers and, in several occasions, she met a skinny, sickly-looking man looking towards the sea. One time she approached him to talk to him, they introduced themselves, but this man, Dionisio Diosdado, only answered with short phrases, yes or no, or nothing at all. Claudia laughed loudly, taking Juan de Dios by surprise. She then told Juan de Dios that one day Dionisio approached her while she was in the plaza next to the towers and told her, nonchalantly, as if he were making dinner plans, that he and her could fall in love, and therefore, they needed to be careful.

"And what happened?" asked a now even more curious Juan de Dios.

"I was surprised and a bit scared, I said nothing to him. And then Dionisio simply turned around and left. Then, I realized that he was the man at the bridge, but because he was out of context, it took me sometime to realized who he was" Claudia stopped for a second. "I just forgot about that incident and I never saw him again, mainly because I stopped going to the bridge" Claudia laughed

Juan de Dios was quiet and pensive. There was a silence.

"So, do you know where could he be?" asked Juan de Dios, knowing the answer.

"As I said, I never saw him again after that episode." Claudia drank her soda.
Claudia looked at him with the intention of ending the meeting. Juan de Dios read her mind.

"I don't want to take more of your time. Please let me ask you one last question. Have you ever heard any of these names before?" Juan de Dios took his little notebook from his shirt pocket and read a few names to Claudia. After hearing some of those names, Claudia became dumbfounded.

"Joaquín Villagrán and Rómulo Ramírez were my boyfriends, but that was a long time ago. Why are you asking me about them? What is all this about? What do they have to do with the missing Diosdado? And what do I have to do with this person at all?" Claudia started to become restless, upset, and scared. Juan de Dios recognized that reaction from Dionisio's manuscript. He hesitated.

"Look, Mrs. Tilapia, I am going to be honest with you, Diosdado's parents found a manuscript, something that Dionisio wrote, and in it these names, and yours, are mentioned. What is the meaning of that? I really do not know. I am as confused as you are."

"Why is this man mentioning my name in his fucking writings or whatever they are?!" Claudia was even more upset.

"I'm going to be honest with you. Dionisio wrote something that resembles his life, your life, with a lot of detail. It probably is just fiction. And in that description appears the names of Joaquín Villagrán and Rómulo Ramírez. That is why we thought that you may know something about Dionisio."

"Has this son of a bitch been spying on me?!" her eyes were now like fire.

"I do not know."

"Then, what does it mean?" yelled Claudia, and the people around turned to look at her.

Juan de Dios shifted uncomfortably on his chair.

"I'm going to be honest with you," was Juan de Dios favorite phrase for this conversation, "Dionisio's parents hired me to find him and I'm trying to do my best with the clues I have. Like you, I am very confused and have a lot of questions about this man and the situation around him. My best guess is that Dionisio researched about your life in detail; how did he do it? Your guess is as good as mine. But he decided to write about you. Why? Maybe he was obsessed, fixated. But it is a mystery."

"You are scaring Mr. De Dios."

"Please believe me that it is not my intention. I would recommend for you to not pay too much attention to all of this and just continue your life as usual."

"What? How can you tell me this? There's a maniac lost in Salamanca, or La Costa, who knows, that is fixated with my life and you tell me not to worry?!"

Claudia stood up quickly and while doing it, bumped the chair, flipping it onto the ground. It was a loud sound. She did not notice it. She turned and left immediately walking northbound in the Boulevard del Mar."

Juan de Dios was shocked. His thoughts were a mess and he could not make sense of anything.

"I found and talked to Claudia Alicante. She knows nothing about your son."

"What do you mean, nothing?" asked Mr. Diosdado.

"I mean, she'd met him on a few occasions, but to her, he was just an acquaintance. She has not seen him in a long time."

"What are we going to do to find my son?" cried a desperate Mrs. Diosdado.

"Don't worry, I will find him." lied Juan de Dios.

When Juan Carlos arrived home, Claudia Tilapia hugged him tight for a long time and did not let him loose until she started crying. Alarmed, Juan Carlos asked her what was wrong, and she told him about her meeting with the private investigator. Juan Carlos did not understand how Claudia was involved in the disappearance of this man. He comforted her and told her not to worry, that he was going to call Juan de Dios to ask him more about Dionisio. Claudia searched in her pockets and found the business card that she handed like a little child to Juan Carlos.

Part 15

"This is the weirdest case I have ever encountered." said Juan de Dios to his friend drinking coffee with him.

"As long as you get paid, who cares?" answered the friend.

"True, but it's very interesting. You tell me, there is this normal person, with a very stable job and suddenly he leaves La Costa. He goes to Salamanca, calls his parents telling him he's now living there and then disappears. Then, the parents and I discovered that this person wrote a manuscript, some sort of story in which the life of a Claudia Alicante is narrated in detail, along with stories about his life. It turns out that Claudia Alicante is a real person, she met Dionisio a few times and forgot about him."

"Dionisio?" asked the friend with curiosity.

"Yes, Dionisio is the missing person. But his name is not important. In the manuscript, there is a detailed explanation of several deaths, some of which are people that Claudia knew at some point. The manuscript even mentions the death of Melinda Ramsden."

"The British? I thought she was missing, not dead." said the friend.

"Yes, the British. And yes, she disappeared but Dionisio writes about her dying in a very creepy way. Anyway, Melinda was living with Mr. and Mrs. Diosdado for a time."

"Diosdado…?" asked the friend.

"Mr. and Mrs. Diosdado are Dionisio's parents."

"You mean Dionisio Diosdado?" asked the friend, but this time as if a light had gone on in his mind.

"Yes."

The friend grabbed the newspaper from his backpack, took it out, scanned through some pages to find the Nation section. He browsed it to find what he was looking for. He showed it to Juan de Dios. The principal investigator read it, but found nothing of relevance.

"What is this?"

"Look at it."

"Yes, it's the news about the murder of a priest in Salamanca. It happened last week. This is old news."

"Look at the photo."

"It is the priest shaking hands with a man."

"For crying out loud! Read the fucking legend."

Juan de Dios eyes opened in surprise.

"It's him!"

"Maybe, it is not a common name."

The legend describes the last photo of Father Rigoberto Verne, taken a few days before his murder. In the photo, there is one of the men staying in the shelter, Dionisio Diosdado. Both are smiling to the camera surrounded by nuns and other homeless persons. In the background, there is the profile of a woman, almost blurry, but showing a very white smile. Juan de Dios had seen this smile before.

Part 16

Many people say that the formations on the surface of the moon facing the earth look like a rabbit. Some have even thought, when seeing the craters through a telescope, that the moon was made of Swiss cheese. But the truth is that the moon is just a sphere of compacted dust, rotating as a servant, around its master Earth. And that night, the servant was shining intensely as if it were the nocturnal version of the sun. From the hospital window, Ricardo Zambrano, a nurse working the night shift, admired the moon on that calm night where nothing seemed to happen. Work was light, patients seemed to be doing great and required little attention. It was a quiet but awkward night. Ricardo Zambrano finished studying the moon and returned to care for his patients. The last room in the corridor of the seventh floor was closed; he knocked to announce his entrance but there was no answer. He entered and looked at the man asleep that was breathing peacefully. He got closer to have a better look, and concluded that the man was doing well. He left the room, and at the time he was about to close the door, The Death snuck in without Ricardo Zambrano noticing her. She stood carefully and gently at the edge of the bed; She did not want to wake him up. She touched his hand and

Dionisio felt Hers cold but recognized it immediately: it was Her hand, that hand that he pretended to unintentionally touch many times just to feel close to Her. The Death smiled at him, a white smile that only old friends can give, but Dionisio did not see it. Their hands caressed each other's, feeling each other, reencountering each other. They talked for some time, not much. Dionisio was tired and with little life left. She started to miss him already. After some time, Dionisio opened his eyes just a little, they were heavy. He looked at Her and remembered the first time he saw Her when he came into this world. The Death smiled at him and caressed his arm tenderly. There was a long silence that to Dionisio seemed like the beginning of eternity. He closed his eyes and The Death removed Her hand from Dionisio's arm. He reopened them and looked directly into Her beautiful eyes, those eyes where he could lose himself for ages. She looked directly at his; his dead eyes. Dionisio nodded and The Death mirrored his movements. Dionisio closed his eyes and never opened them again. His heart, finally, rested.

Ricardo Zambrano took Dionisio's body to the morgue. He greeted the staff in charge and left his load there. The death certificate indicated that Dionisio Diosdado had died of cardiac failure at the age of 34. He was the only death reported in Salamanca for a month. She was mourning.

Part 17

When Mr. and Mrs. Diosdado and Juan de Dios arrived in Salamanca, Dionisio had been dead for seven days and the hospital was ready to donate his body to science. His parents cried bitterly. They collected his filthy clothes. They decided not to transport Dionisio's body to La Costa and instead they buried him in Salamanca, saying that he was born there and he died there as well. The funeral was very simple, only the Diosdados and Juan de Dios were present.

They sold all of Dionisio's belongings that remained in La Costa, but saved the manuscript in an old cabinet where it was forgotten and turned yellow and moldy with the years. No one else read it. One year after Dionisio's death, the Diosdados moved to Salamanca, remembering until their last days the son that had left them too early. Mrs. Diosdado died eight years after Dionisio, and a month later Mr. Diosdado followed her.

Part 18

Juan de Dios stayed in Salamanca for a couple more weeks after they found Dionisio. During those two weeks, he could not stop thinking about him, Claudia, and all of the other people named in his manuscript that had died as Dionisio's writing had indicated. Juan de Dios was curious and decided to continue this investigation on his own. When he drove back to La Costa, he stopped at a gas station to refuel before the long trip. He got out of his car to find a public phone. When he found one, he took his little notebook from his shirt pocket and called Claudia Tilapia. After the fourth beep, he was ready to hang up when Claudia's voice answered. Juan de Dios sighed and for a couple of seconds said nothing. Claudia repeated her *hello*, and when Juan de Dios heard her, he reacted. He introduced himself and rapidly said that Dionisio Diosdado had died a couple of weeks ago in Salamanca. Claudia expelled an *oh, my God!* and thanked Juan de Dios for the courtesy call. Juan Carlos, beside her, listened to Juan de Dios' words spilling over the telephone. He felt himself smiling, as if a heavy load had been removed.

Juan de Dios got in his car and continued his trip back to La Costa. We drove hundreds of miles while the sadness and pain that he saw in the Diosdados' faces inundated his mind, and he could not stop thinking about the many unanswered questions they had. Tears came to his eyes and suddenly he found himself weeping. He needed to stop the car to regain control of himself. He pulled over. He opened the window to breathe the night's air but it was not sufficient. He decided to get out of the car, still with his eyes full of tears. And when he did, he did not see the semi-truck dangerously approaching him. When he noticed it, it was too late: the last thing he saw was the headlights of the truck, and after that, he felt the immense pain of the truck hitting his body and crushing most of his bones, almost liquefying all of his internal organs. Juan de Dios died fast.

That same night, Claudia Tilapia, with a sweaty body alit Juan Carlos' waist, and rested naked close to him on her side of the bed. The air was full of the scent of oranges and she was content. She closed her eyes, she was tired, and she lost herself in a deep sleep. In her dreams, she was in a large valley surrounded by enormous mountainous peaks growing powerfully. The snow started to fall and far away she could see a buffalo trotting gingerly. She looked to the opposite side, towards the horizon, and she saw him. She waved at him with her hand. He returned the greeting and both smiled at each other as old friends do. After this, he disappeared in the snow that was now heavily falling. Claudia Tilapia looked down and noticed that the snow was already covering her naked legs, drowning her up all the way to her knees.

The end

www.ingramcontent.com/pod-product-compliance
Lightning Source LLC
Chambersburg PA
CBHW052002150726
47999CB00004B/1487